ALSO BY CHARLAINE HARRIS

A Fool and His Honey
Shakespeare's Christmas
Shakespeare's Champion
Dead over Heels
Shakespeare's Landlord
The Julius House
Three Bedrooms, One Corpse
A Bone to Pick
Real Murders
A Secret Rage
Sweet and Deadly

Shakespeare's Trollop

Shakespeare's Trollop

Charlaine Harris

St. Martin's Minotaur ✹ New York

www.minotaurbooks.com

Library of Congress Cataloging-in-Publication Data

Harris, Charlaine.
    Shakespeare's trollop / Charlaine Harris.—1st ed.
        p.   cm.
    ISBN 0-312-26228-0
    1. Bard, Lily (Fictitious character)—Fiction. 2. Women cleaning personnel—Fiction. 3. Arkansas—Fiction. I. Title.
PS3558.A6427 S54   2000
813'54—dc21   00-029687

First Edition: August 2000

10 9 8 7 6 5 4 3 2 1

This book is dedicated to my other family, the people of St. James Episcopal Church. They are at liberty to be horrified by its contents.

ACKNOWLEDGMENTS

My thanks to the usual suspects: Drs. Aung and Tammy Than and former police chief Phil Gates. My further thanks to an American icon, John Walsh.

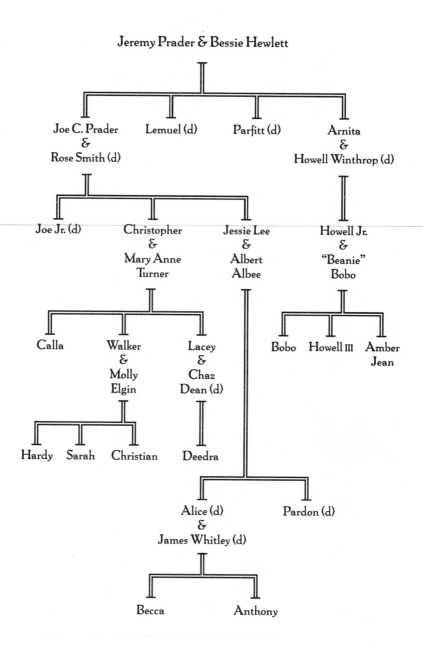

ONE

By the time I opened my eyes and yawned that morning, she had been sitting in the car in the woods for seven hours. Of course, I didn't know that, didn't even know Deedra was missing. No one did.

If no one realizes a person is missing, is she gone?

While I brushed my teeth and drove to the gym, dew must have been glistening on the hood of her car. Since Deedra had been left leaning toward the open window on the driver's side, perhaps there was dew on her cheek, too.

As the people of Shakespeare read morning papers, showered, prepared school lunches for their children, and let their dogs out for a morning's commune with nature, Deedra was becoming part of nature herself—deconstructing, returning to her components. Later, when the sun warmed up the forest, there were flies. Her makeup looked ghastly, since the skin underlying it was changing color. Still she sat, unmoving, unmoved: life changing all around her, evolving constantly, and Deedra lifeless at its center, all her choices gone. The changes she would make from now on were involuntary.

One person in Shakespeare knew where Deedra was. One person knew that she was missing from her normal setting, in fact, missing from her life itself. And that person was waiting, waiting for some unlucky Arkansan—a hunter, a birdwatcher, a surveyor—to find Deedra, to set in motion the business of recording the circumstances of her permanent absence.

That unlucky citizen would be me.

If the dogwoods hadn't been blooming, I wouldn't have been looking at the trees. If I hadn't been looking at the trees, I wouldn't have seen the flash of red down the unmarked road to the right. Those little unmarked roads—more like tracks—are so common in rural Arkansas that they're not worth a second glance. Usually they lead to deer hunters' camps, or oil wells, or back into the property of someone who craves privacy *deeply*. But the dogwood I glimpsed, perhaps twenty feet into the woods, was beautiful, its flowers glowing like pale butterflies among the dark branchless trunks of the slash pines. So I slowed down to look, and caught a glimpse of red down the track, and in so doing started the tiles falling in a certain pattern.

All the rest of my drive out to Mrs. Rossiter's, and while I cleaned her pleasantly shabby house and bathed her reluctant spaniel, I thought about that flash of bright color. It hadn't been the brilliant carmine of a cardinal, or the soft purplish shade of an azalea, but a glossy metallic red, like the paint on a car.

In fact, it had been the exact shade of Deedra Dean's Taurus. There were lots of red cars in Shakespeare, and some of them were Tauruses. As I dusted Mrs. Rossiter's den, I scorned myself for fretting about Deedra Dean, who was chronologically and biologically a woman. Deedra did not expect or require me to worry about her and I didn't need any more problems than I already had.

That afternoon, Mrs. Rossiter provided a stream-of-consciousness commentary to my work. She, at least, was just as always: plump, sturdy, kind, curious, and centered on the old spaniel, Durwood. I wondered from time to time how Mr. Rossiter had felt about this when he'd been alive. Maybe Mrs. Rossiter had become so fixated on Durwood since her husband had died? I'd never known M. T. Rossiter, who had departed this world over four years ago, around the time I'd landed in Shakespeare. While I knelt in the bathroom, using the special rinse attachment to flush the shampoo out of Durwood's coat, I interrupted Mrs. Rossiter's monologue on next month's Garden Club flower show to ask her what her husband had been like.

Since I'd stopped her midflow, it took Birdie Rossiter a moment to redirect the stream of conversation.

"Well . . . my husband . . . it's so strange you should ask, I was just thinking of him. . . ."

Birdie Rossiter had always just been thinking of whatever topic you suggested.

"M. T. was a farmer."

I nodded, to show I was listening. I'd spotted a flea in the water swirling down the drain and I was hoping Mrs. Rossiter wouldn't see it. If she did, Durwood and I would have to go through various unpleasant processes.

"He farmed all his life, he came from a farming family. He never knew anything else but country. His mother actually chewed tobacco, Lily! Can you imagine? But she was good woman, Miss Audie, with a good heart. When I married M. T.—I was just eighteen—Miss Audie told us to build a house wherever on their land we pleased. Wasn't that nice? So M. T. picked this site, and we spent a year working on the floor plan. And it turned out to be an ordinary old house, after all that planning!" Birdie laughed. Under the fluorescent light of the bathroom, the threads of gray in the darkness of her hair shone so brightly they looked painted.

By the time Birdie had reached the point in her husband's biography where M. T. was asked to join the Gospellaires, a men's quartet at Mt. Olive Baptist, I had begun my next grocery list, at least in my head.

An hour later, I was saying good-bye, Mrs. Rossiter's check tucked in the pocket of my blue jeans.

"See you next Monday afternoon," she said, trying to sound offhand instead of lonely. "We'll have our work cut out for us then, because it'll be the day before I have the prayer luncheon."

I wondered if she would want me to put bows on Durwood's ears again, like I had the last time Birdie had hosted the prayer luncheon. The spaniel and I exchanged glances. Luckily for me, Durwood was the kind of dog who didn't hold a grudge. I nodded, grabbed up my caddy of cleaning products and rags, and retreated before Mrs. Rossiter could think of something else to talk about. It was time to get to my next job, Camille Emerson's. I gave Durwood a farewell pat on the head as I opened the front door. "He's looking good," I offered. Durwood's poor health and bad eyesight were a never-ending worry to his owner. A few months before, he'd tripped Birdie with his leash and she'd broken her arm, but that hadn't lessened her attachment to the dog.

"I think he's good as gold," Birdie told me, her voice firm. She stood on her front porch watching me as I put my supplies in the car and slid into the driver's seat. She laboriously squatted down by Durwood and made the dog raise his paw and wave good-bye to me. I lifted my hand: I knew from experience that she wouldn't stop Durwood's farewell until I responded.

As I thought about what I had to do next, I was almost tempted to turn off the engine and sit longer, listening to the ceaseless stream of Birdie Rossiter's talk. But I started the car, backed out of her driveway, and looked both ways several times before venturing out. There wasn't much traffic on Farm Hill Road, but what there was tended to be fast and careless.

I knew that when I drew opposite the unmarked road, I would stop on the narrow grassy shoulder. My window was open. When I cut my engine, the silence took over. I heard . . . nothing.

I got out and closed the door behind me. A breeze lifted my short, curly hair and made my T-shirt feel inadequate. I shivered. The tingling feeling at the back of my neck was warning me to drive off but sometimes, I guess, you just can't dodge the bullet.

My sneakers made small squeaky noises on the worn blacktop as I crossed the road. Deep in the woods to the west, I heard a bobwhite sound its cry. Not a car was in sight.

After a second's hesitation I entered the woods, following the unmarked road. It hardly deserved the name.

It was really two bare tracks with grass growing up between them, some old gravel pressed down into the ground marking where the last load had been leveled years before. My progress was quiet, but not silent, and I slowed involuntarily. The path curved slightly to the right, and as I rounded that curve I saw the source of the flash of color.

It was a car—a Taurus—parked facing away from Farm Hill Road.

Someone was sitting in the front seat. I could see a head outlined on the driver's side. I stopped dead in my tracks. My skin rose in goose bumps up and down my arms. If I'd been apprehensive before, now I was truly frightened. Somehow, that unexpected glimpse of another human being was more shocking than the discovery that a car was parked out here in the woods where it had no business parking.

"Hello?" I said quietly.

But the person in the front seat of the red Taurus did not move.

Suddenly I found I was too scared to say anything else. The woods seemed to close in around me. The silence had taken on an oppressive life of its own. "Bob—*white!*" shrieked the bird, and I nearly leapt out of my skin.

I stood stock-still and fought a fierce internal battle. More than anything, I wanted to walk away from this car with its silent occupant—wanted to forget I'd ever been here.

I couldn't.

Despising my indecision, I marched up to the car and bent to look in.

For a moment I was distracted by her nakedness, by the bareness of breasts and thighs, by the alien protrusion between her legs. But when I looked into the face of the woman in the car, I had to bite my lower lip to keep from crying out. Deedra's eyes were halfway open, but they weren't returning my gaze.

I made myself acknowledge what I was seeing and smelling—the deadness of her—and then I let myself snap back up straight and move a step away from the car. I stood gasping until I felt steadier, thinking of what I should do next.

Another alien color, not natural to these greening woods, caught the corner of my eye and I began to look around me, trying not to move. In fact, I was hardly breathing in my effort to make no imprint on the scene around me.

The biggest patch of color was a cream-colored blouse tossed over a thorny vine that had woven itself between two trees. A few feet from that was a black skirt, cut narrow and short. It was on the ground, and it was as crumpled as the blouse. A pair of pantyhose and—what was that? I leaned over to see more clearly, making an effort to satisfy my curiosity without moving my feet. Deedra's pearls. The pantyhose and pearls were festooned over a low branch. I was missing the bra, which I eventually located hanging from a bush, and the shoes, which had been thrown separately some feet farther down the trail. Black leather pumps. That left the purse. I almost leaned over again to see if it was in the car, but instead I replayed the scene in my mind. The purse wasn't in the front seat of Deedra's car; she would've been carrying the little black leather shoulder-strap bag she usually used with the pumps. You don't work for someone as long as I'd worked for Deedra without knowing her clothes and her habits.

So I wouldn't have to decide what to do about this for a few more seconds, I looked hard for the purse, but I didn't spot it. Either it had been tossed farther than her clothes, or the person in the woods with her had taken it with him.

With Deedra it was always a "him."

I took a deep breath and braced myself, knowing what I had to do and admitting it to myself. I had to call the sheriff's department. I took one more look around, feeling the shock of the scene all over again, and patted my cheeks. But there were no tears.

Deedra was not someone you cried over, I realized as I walked swiftly out of the woods to the road. Deedra's was a shake-your-head death—not entirely unanticipated, within the realm of possibility. Since Deedra had been in her twenties, the mere fact that she was dead should have been shocking, but there again . . . it wasn't.

As I punched the number for the sheriff's department (the cell phone had been a Christmas surprise from Jack Leeds) I felt regret about my lack of amazement. The death of anyone young and healthy should be outrageous. But I knew, as I told the dispatcher where I was—right outside the Shakespeare city limit, in fact I could see the sign from where I stood—that very few people would truly be stunned about Deedra Dean being naked, violated, and dead in a car in the woods.

Of all the people in the world, I would be the last one to blame the victim for the crime. But it was simply undeniable that Deedra had thrown herself into the victim pool with vigor, even eagerness. She must have considered her family's money and social position life jacket enough.

After tossing the cell phone back into my car through the open window, I leaned against the hood and wondered what situation had led to Deedra's death. When a woman has many sexual partners, the chance of her falling foul of one of them escalates, and I was assuming that was what had happened. I mulled over that assumption. If Deedra had worked in a factory that employed mostly men, would she be more likely to die than a woman who worked in a factory that employed mostly women? I had no idea. I wondered if a promiscuous man was more likely to be murdered than a chaste man.

I was actually happy to see the sheriff's car rounding the corner. I hadn't met the new sheriff, though I'd seen her around town. As Marta Schuster emerged from her official car, I crossed the road once again.

We shook hands, and she gave me the silent eyes-up-and-down evaluation that was supposed to prove to me that she was tough and impartial.

I took the opportunity to scan her, too.

Marta's father, Marty Schuster, had been elected county sheriff for many terms. When he'd died on the job last year, Marta had been appointed to fill in the remainder of his term of office. Marty had been a genuinely tough little bantamweight of a man, but his wife must have been made of sterner and more majestic stuff. Marta was a Valkyrie of a woman. She was robust, blond, and very fair complexioned, like many people in this area. Shakespeare had been founded by a literature-loving, homesick Englishman, but in the late eighteen hundreds the little town had had an influx of German immigrants.

The sheriff was small-bosomed and somewhat thick-waisted, which the uniform blouse and skirt did nothing but accentuate. Marta Schuster was somewhere in her mid-thirties, about my age.

"You're Lily Bard, who called in the death?"

"Yes."

"The body is . . . ?"

"In there." I pointed toward the little track.

Another sheriff's department car pulled in behind Marta Schuster's. The man who got out was tall, really tall, maybe six-four or more. I wondered if the sheriff's department had height restrictions, and if so how this man had gotten in. He looked like a brick wall in his uniform, and he was as fair-skinned as Marta, though his hair was dark—what there was of it. He was of the shaved-head school of law enforcement.

"Stay here," Marta Schuster told me brusquely. She pointed to the bumper of her official vehicle. She went to the trunk, unlocked it, and pulled out a pair of sneakers. She slipped off her pumps and put on the sneakers. She wasn't happy about being in a skirt, I could tell; she hadn't known when she got to work that morning that she'd be called on to tromp around in the woods. The sheriff got a few more items out of her car and went to the edge of the trees. Marta Schuster was visibly bracing herself to remember every lesson she'd ever learned about homicide investigation.

I looked at my watch and tried not to sigh. It seemed likely that I would be late for Camille Emerson's.

When she'd finished preparing herself mentally, Marta made a gesture like ones I'd seen on TV in old westerns, where the head of the cavalry troop is ready to move out. You know, he raises his gloved hand and motions forward, without looking back. That was exactly the gesture Marta used, and the deputy obeyed it silently. I expected her to toss him a Milk Bone.

I was grabbing at any mental straw to avoid thinking of the body in the car, but I knew that I'd have to face it sooner or later. No matter what Deedra's life had been, or how I'd felt about her choices in that life, I discovered I was genuinely sorry that she was dead. And her mother! I winced when I thought of Lacey Dean Knopp's reaction to her only child's death. Lacey had always seemed oblivious of her daughter's activities, and I'd never known if that was self-protective or Deedra-protective. Either way, I kind of admired it.

My calm time ended when a third vehicle pulled over to the shoulder, this one a battered Subaru. A young man, blond and blocky, leapt from the driver's seat and looked around wildly. His eyes passed over me as if I were one of the trees. When the young man spotted the opening into the woods, he threw himself along the narrow shoulder like a novice skier hurls himself down a slope, apparently intending to dash down the road to the scene of Deedra's demise.

He was in civilian clothes, and I didn't know him. I was betting he had no business at the crime scene. But I wasn't the law. I let him pass, though I'd stopped leaning against the sheriff's car and uncrossed my arms.

At that moment Marta Schuster came back into sight and yelled, "No, Marlon!" The big deputy dogging her stepped around her neatly, grabbed the smaller man's shoulders, and held him fast. I'd seen the smaller man around the apartments, I recalled, and I realized for the first time that this boy was Marlon Schuster, Marta's brother. My stomach clenched at this bombshell of a complication.

"Marlon," the sheriff said in a harsh voice. It would've stopped me. "Marlon, get ahold of yourself."

"Is it true? Is it her?"

From only five feet away, I could hardly avoid hearing this conversation.

Marta took a deep breath. "Yes, it's Deedra," she said, quite gently, and motioned to the deputy, who let go of the boy's arm.

To my amazement, the young man drew back that arm to swing at his sister. The deputy had turned to walk to his car, and Marta Schuster seemed too astounded to defend herself, so I covered the ground and seized his cocked right arm. The ungrateful fool swung around and went for me with his left. Well, I too had a free hand, and I struck him—*seiken*, a thrust—right in the solar plexus.

He made a sound like "oof" as the air left him, and then went down on his knees. I released him and stepped away. He wouldn't be bothering anyone for a few minutes.

"Idiot," the sheriff said, crouching down by him. The deputy was right by me, suddenly, his hand playing nervously around his gun. I wondered which of us he'd draw on. After a second his hand relaxed, and I did too.

"Where'd you learn that?" asked the deputy. I looked up at him. He had bitter-chocolate brown eyes.

"Karate class," I said, throwing it away, not wanting to talk about it. Marshall Sedaka, my *sensei*, would be pleased.

"You're that woman," the deputy said.

All of a sudden, I felt real tired. "I'm Lily Bard," I

12

said, keeping my voice neutral. "And if you all are through with me, I need to be getting to my next job."

"Just tell me again how you happened to find her," Marta Schuster said, leaving her brother to fend for himself. She looked sideways at her deputy. He nodded. They seemed to be good at nonverbal communication. She addressed me again. "Then you can go, long as we know where to reach you."

I gave her the Joe-Friday facts: Mrs. Rossiter's phone number, my cell phone number, my home phone number, and where I'd be working this afternoon if I ever got to leave this stretch of road.

"And you knew the deceased how?" she asked again, as if that was a point she hadn't quite gotten straight in her head.

"I cleaned her place. I live next to her apartment building," I said.

"How long had you worked for Deedra?"

The tall deputy had gone down the path with a camera after making sure that Marlon was off his tear. The sheriff's brother had recovered enough to haul himself up to the hood of his Subaru. He was sprawled over it, weeping, his head buried in his hands. His sister completely ignored him, though he was making a considerable amount of noise.

Two more deputies arrived in another squad car and emerged with rolls of crime-scene tape, and Marta Schuster interrupted me to give them directions.

"I worked for Deedra—though I'm sure her mother subsidized her—for over three years," I said, when the sheriff turned her attention back to me. "I cleaned Deedra's apartment once a week."

"So, you were friendly with her?"

"No." That didn't require any thought.

"Yet you knew her for more than three years," Marta Schuster observed, pretending to be surprised.

I shrugged. "She was most often gone to work while I was at her place." Though sometimes she was still there; and sometimes the men would still be there, but the sheriff hadn't asked me about the men. She would, though.

While the sheriff gave more directions to her deputies, I had a little time to think. The pictures! I closed my eyes to contain my dismay.

One of the least explicable things about Deedra was her fondness for nude pictures of herself. She'd kept a little pile of them in her lingerie drawer for years. Every time I'd put her clean clothes away, I'd felt an uncomfortable stab of disapproval. Of all the things Deedra did to parade her vulnerability, this was the thing I found most distasteful.

I thought of those pictures lying out on a desk in the sheriff's office, being viewed by all and sundry. I felt a wave of regret, an almost overwhelming impulse to rush to Deedra's apartment ahead of the law, remove the pictures, and burn them.

Marlon Schuster slammed his hand against the hood of his car, and his sister, who was watching my face rather than his, jumped. I carefully avoided her eyes. Marlon needed to take his display of grief to another, more discreet, location.

"So, you have a key to the apartment?" Marty Schuster asked.

"I do," I said promptly. "And I'm going to give it to

14

you now." I abandoned any quixotic notion of shielding Deedra's true nature from the men and women examining her death. I was sure almost everyone in town had heard that Deedra was free with herself. But would they look for her killer as hard, once they'd seen those pictures? Would they keep their mouths shut, so rumors didn't reach Deedra's mother?

I pressed my lips together firmly. There was nothing I could do, I told myself sternly. Deedra was on her own. I'd set the investigation of her death in motion, but beyond that, I couldn't help her. The cost to myself would be too high.

So thinking, I worked her key off the ring and dropped it in the open palm of Sheriff Marta Schuster. A vague memory stirred, and I wondered if I knew of another key. Yes, I recalled, Deedra kept an emergency key in her stall in the apartment carport. As I opened my mouth to tell the sheriff about this key, she made a chopping gesture to cut off my comment. I shrugged. But I told myself that this was truly my only key, and that because I'd turned over this key, Deedra Dean was out of my life.

"I'll need a list of the people you've seen there," Sheriff Schuster said sharply. She was aching to return to the crime scene, her face turning often to the woods.

I'd already begun to go back to my car. I didn't like being hushed with that chopping hand, it wasn't like I chattered. And I didn't like being ordered.

"I never saw anyone there," I said, my back to the sheriff.

"You . . . in the years you cleaned her apartment, you never saw anyone else there?" Marta Schuster's tone let me know she was well aware of Deedra's reputation.

"Her stepfather was there one morning when Deedra was having car trouble."

"And that's all?" Marta Schuster asked, openly disbelieving.

"That's all." Marlon, of course, had been creeping out of there three or four days ago, but she knew about him already and it didn't seem the time to bring that up again.

"That's a little surprising."

I half-turned, shrugging. "You through with me?"

"No. I want you to meet me at the apartment in about two hours. Since you're familiar with Deedra's belongings, you can tell us if anything's missing or not. It would be better if Mrs. Knopp didn't have to do it, I'm sure you agree."

I felt trapped. There was nothing I could say besides, "I'll be there."

My involvement in the troubled life of Deedra Dean was not yet over.

TWO

Camille Emerson would hate me later for not telling her my little news item, but I just didn't want to talk about Deedra's death. Camille was on her way out, anyway, a list clutched in her plump hand.

"I remembered to put the clean sheets out this time," she said with a touch of pride. I nodded, not willing to give a grown woman a pat on the back for doing a simple thing like putting out clean sheets for me to change. Camille Emerson was cheerful and untidy. Though I didn't dislike her—in fact, I felt glad to work for her—Camille was trying to warm up our relationship into some kind of facsimile of friendship, and I found that as irritating as the employers who treated me like a slave.

"See you later!" Camille said finally, giving up on a response. After a second I said, "Good-bye." It was lucky I was in a mood to work hard, since the Emersons had made more than their usual mess since my last visit. There were only four of them (Camille, her husband, Cooper, their two boys) but each Emerson was determined to live in the center of chaos. After spending fifteen minutes one day trying to sort out the different sizes of sheets I needed, I'd suggested to Camille that she leave the clean sheets on each bed, ready for me to change. That was much better than extending my time there, since Mondays were always busy for me, and Camille had blanched at the thought of paying me more. We were both happy with the result; that is, when Camille remembered her part.

My cell phone rang while I was drying the newly scrubbed sink in the hall bathroom.

"Yes?" I said cautiously. I still wasn't used to carrying this phone.

"Hi."

"Jack." I could feel myself smiling. I grabbed my mop and cleaning materials in their caddy, awkwardly because of the telephone, and moved down the hall to the kitchen.

"Where are you?"

"Camille Emerson's."

"Are you alone?"

"Yes."

"I've got news." Jack sounded half excited, half uneasy.

"What?"

"I'm catching a plane in an hour."

"For?" He was supposed to be coming to stay with me tonight.

"I'm working on a fraud case. The main suspect left last night for Sacramento."

I was even more miserable than I'd been after finding Deedra's body. I'd looked forward to Jack's visit so much. I'd even changed my sheets and come home from the gym early this morning to make sure my own little house was spanking clean. The disappointment bit into me.

"Lily?"

"I'm here."

"I'm sorry."

"You have to work," I said, my voice flat and even. "I'm just . . ." Angry, unhappy, empty; all of the above.

"I'm going to miss you, too."

"Will you?" I asked, my voice as low as if there were someone there to hear me. "Will you think of me when you're alone in your hotel room?"

He allowed as how he would.

We talked a little longer. Though I got satisfaction out of realizing that Jack really would regret he wasn't with me, the end result was the same; I wouldn't see him for a week, at the very least, and two weeks was more realistic.

After we hung up I realized I hadn't told him about finding Deedra dead. I wasn't going to phone him back. Our good-byes had been said. He'd met Deedra, but that was about the extent of his knowledge of her . . . as far as I knew. He'd lived across the hall from her before I'd met him, I recalled with a surge of uneasiness. But I channeled it aside, unwilling to worry about a faint possibility that Jack had enjoyed Deedra's offerings before he'd met me. I shrugged. I'd tell him about her death the next time we talked.

I tugged the crammed garbage bag out of the can, yanked the ties together in a knot, and braced myself as Camille Emerson staggered through the kitchen door, laden with grocery bags and good will.

I was late for my appointment with Marta Schuster, but I didn't care. I'd parked my car in my own carport before striding next door to the eight-unit apartment building, noticing as I threw open the big front door that there were two sheriff's department vehicles parked at the curb. I was in a bad mood, a truculent mood—not the frame of mind best for dealing with law-enforcement officials.

"Take a breath," advised a cool, familiar, voice.

It was good advice, and I stopped to take it.

"Marta Schuster and her storm trooper are up there," Becca Whitley went on, stepping from her apartment doorway at the back of the hall to stand by the foot of the stairs.

Becca Whitley was a wet dream about three years past its prime. She had very long blond hair, very bright blue eyes, strong (if miniature) features, and cone-shaped breasts thrusting out from an athletic body. Becca, who'd lived in Shakespeare for about five months, had inherited the apartment building from her uncle, Pardon Albee, and she lived in his old apartment.

I'd never thought Becca would last even this long in little Shakespeare; she'd told me she'd moved here from Dallas, and she seemed like a city kind of woman. I'd been sure she'd put the building up for sale and take off for some urban center. She'd surprised me by staying.

And she'd taken my place as the highest-ranking student in Marshall's class.

But there were moments I felt a connection to Becca, and this was one of them. We'd begun a tentative sort of friendship.

"How long have they been up there?" I asked.

"Hours." Becca looked up the stairs as if, through the floors and doors, she could watch what the sheriff was so busy doing. "Did they tell you to come?"

"Yes."

"What about Marlon?"

"He was at the crime scene bawling his eyes out."

"Ew." Becca scrunched her nose in distaste. "He's the one been seeing her so hot and heavy."

I nodded. I wondered how well the sheriff would investigate her own brother.

"Do you have your key?" Becca asked.

"I gave it to them."

"Good move," she said. "They got my copy of her key, too."

I shifted from foot to foot. "I better go up. I'm supposed to tell them if anything's missing."

"See you tonight," she called after me, and I lifted my hand in acknowledgment.

Deedra's apartment was the right rear, just above Becca's. It overlooked the paved rear parking lot, not an inspiring view. It held a carport divided into eight stalls, a Dumpster, and not much else. I wasn't sure who, besides Deedra, lived on the second floor now, but I'd known many of the people who'd passed through. Claude Friedrich, the chief of police and a friend of mine, had moved from the second floor to the first after a leg injury. I figured he and Deedra had been the in the building the longest. Generally, the eight units of the so-called Shakespeare Garden Apartments stayed full because the units were a nice size and fairly reasonable. I was pretty sure Becca had gone up on the rent as the leases ran out, because I had a faint memory of Deedra complaining, but it hadn't been an outrageous increase.

I knocked on Deedra's door. The same tall officer answered, the guy who'd been at the crime scene. He filled up the doorway; after a long second, he stepped aside so I could enter. He was lucky looking at me was a free activity, or he would be broke by now.

"Sheriff's in there," he said, pointing toward Deedra's bedroom. But instead of following his hint, I stood in the center of the living room and looked around. I'd been in to clean the past Friday, and today was Monday, so the place still looked good; Deedra was careless with herself, but she had always been fairly tidy with everything else.

The furniture seemed to be in the same spots, and all the cushions were straight. Her television and VCR were untouched; rows of videotapes sat neat and square on their little bookcase by the television. The brand-new CD player was on the stand by the television. All Deedra's magazines were in the neat stack I'd arranged a few days before, except for a new issue left open on the coffee table in front of the couch, where Deedra usually sat when she watched television. Her bills were piled in the shallow basket where she'd tossed them.

"Notice anything different?" The tall deputy was standing by the door and keeping quiet, a point in his favor.

I shook my head and resumed my examination.

"Emanuel," he said suddenly.

Was this some kind of religious statement? My eyebrows drew in and I regarded him with some doubt.

"Clifton Emanuel."

After a distinct pause, I understood. "You're Clifton Emanuel," I said tentatively. He nodded.

I didn't need to know his name, but he wanted me to know it. Maybe he was a celebrity freak, True Crime Division, Famous Victims Subsection. Like Sharon Tate, but alive.

Maybe he was just being polite.

I was relieved when the sheriff stuck her head out of Deedra's bedroom and jerked it back in a motion that told me I'd better join her.

"Everything in the living room okay?" she asked.

"Yes."

"What about this room?"

I stood at the foot of Deedra's bed and turned around slowly. Deedra had loved jewelry, and it was everywhere; necklaces, earrings, bracelets, an anklet or two. The impression was that the jewelry was strewn around, but if you looked closer, you would notice that the backs were on the earrings and the earrings were in pairs. The necklaces were lain straight and fastened so they wouldn't tangle. That was normal. Some of the drawers were not completely shut—there again, that was typical Deedra. The bed was made quite tidily; it was queen-size, with a high, carved headboard that dominated the room. I lifted the corner of the flowered bedspread and peered beneath it.

"Different sheets than I put on last Friday," I said.

"Does that mean something?"

"Means someone slept in it with her since then."

"Did she ever wash the sheets and put them right back on the bed?"

"She never washed anything, especially sheets. She had seven sets. I did her laundry."

Marta Schuster looked startled. Then she looked disgusted. "So if I count the sheet sets in the laundry hamper,

I'll come up with the number of times she entertained since last Friday morning?"

I sighed, hating knowing these things about someone else, much less revealing them. But it was the nature of my job. "Yes," I said wearily.

"Did she have a video camera? I noticed all the tapes out there."

"Yes, she did. She kept it up there, on the closet shelf." I pointed, and Marta fetched. She opened the soft black case, removed the camera, turned it on, and opened the tape bay. Empty.

"Who paid you to clean this place?" she asked out of the blue.

"I thought we'd covered that. Her mother, Lacey, gave Deedra the money so she could afford me."

"Deedra get along with her mother?"

"Yes."

"What about her stepfather?"

I considered my answer. I'd heard a fight between the two so intense I'd considered intervening, maybe three or four months ago. I didn't like Jerrell Knopp. But it was one thing not to like him, another thing to tell the sheriff words he'd spoken in anger.

"They weren't close," I said cautiously.

"Ever see them fight?"

I turned away, began putting Deedra's earrings into her special compartmented box.

"Stop," the sheriff said sharply.

I dropped the pair I was holding as if they'd burst into flames. "Sorry," I said, shaking my head at my own error. "It was automatic." I hoped Marta Schuster stayed diverted.

24

"She always have this much jewelry lying around?"

"Yes." I was relieved she'd asked a question so easily answered. I couldn't stop myself from glancing over at Deedra's chest of drawers, wondering if Marta Schuster had already found the pictures. I wondered whether mentioning them would help in some way.

"They're in my pocket," she said quietly.

My eyes met hers. "Good."

"What do you know about her sex life?"

I could see that this was supposed to signal a trade-off. My mouth twisted in distaste. "Your brother was mighty interested in Deedra, from what I could see. Ask him."

Marta Schuster's hard, square hand shot out and gripped my wrist. "He's just the latest in her long string," she said, her jaw as rigid as the grip of her hand. "He's so new to her that he's dumb enough to be sorry she's dead."

I looked down at her fingers and took slow breaths. I met her eyes again. "Let go of me," I told her in a very careful voice.

Keeping her eyes on my face, she did. Then she took a step away. But she said, "I'm waiting."

"You already know that Deedra was promiscuous. If a man was willing, she was, with very few exceptions."

"Name some names."

"No. It would take too long. Besides, they were almost always gone when I got here." That was my first lie.

"What about the exceptions? She turn anyone down?"

I thought that over. "That kid who worked at the loading dock over at Winthrop Lumber and Supply," I said reluctantly.

"Danny Boyce? Yeah, he's out on parole now. Who else?"

"Dedford Jinks."

"With the city police?" she asked, incredulity written all over her face. "He must be in his fifties."

"So he doesn't want sex?" What universe did Marta Schuster inhabit?

"He's married," Marta protested. Then she flushed red. "Forget I said that."

I shrugged, tired of being in this room with this woman. "He was separated from his wife. But Deedra didn't go with married men."

The sheriff looked openly skeptical. "Anyone else?"

I actually had a helpful memory. "She'd had trouble with someone calling her." Deedra had mentioned that to me the last time I'd cleaned the apartment, just this past Friday. She'd been running late for work, as she all too often did. "Last Friday, she told me that she was getting calls at two or three in the morning. Really nasty calls from a guy . . . somehow disguising his voice, talking about sexual torture."

I could see Deedra, sitting on the end of the very bed we stood by now, easing up her pantyhose and sliding her narrow feet into brown low-heeled pumps. Deedra's head, crowned by its sexily tousled and newly red hair, had been bent to her task, but Deedra kept her head tucked quite a bit anyway to minimize her sharply receding chin, without a doubt her worst feature. She'd stood and scanned herself in the mirror, tugging at the top of the beige suit she thought appropriate for her job in the courthouse. A typical Deedra selection, the suit was just a bit too tight, a smidge too short, and a half-inch too low in the neckline.

Deedra had leaned over to peer into the mirror to apply her lipstick. Her dresser, with its triple mirror, was literally covered with bottles and plastic cases of makeup. Deedra was a virtuoso with foundation, rouge, and eye shadow. She'd had a real gift for it, for using cosmetics to make her look her very best with every outfit she wore. She'd studied the human face and the alterations and illusions a skilled applicator could effect.

I could still see how Deedra had looked as she'd half-turned to tell me what the caller had proposed to do to her; her lower lip a glossy peach and her upper lip bare, her clothes and hair and demeanor just a careful step away from floozy.

"Did she say who she thought he was, the man calling her?"

I shook my head. "Can you check her phone records?" I asked.

"It'll take a while, but we'll get 'em," Marta said.

Her deputy stuck his head into the room. "I've finished searching the bathroom," Emanuel said, his eyes scanning us curiously. "What now?"

"Extra bedroom," the sheriff said. "And bag the sheets on the top of the washer."

His head vanished.

"What about him?" I asked.

"What?" she said, as if she was about to get angry.

"Did he know Deedra?"

Her face changed, then, and I knew she was involved with Clifton Emanuel to some degree.

"I don't know," she said. "But I'll find out."

. . .

Janet Shook aimed a kick at my stomach, and I arched back to dodge it. My hand shot out and gripped her ankle, and then I had her.

"Stop!" called a commanding voice. "Okay, what are you going to do now, Janet?" our *sensei* continued. He was leaning against the mirrored wall, his arms folded across his chest.

We had frozen in position, Janet balancing easily on one foot, my fingers still circling her ankle. The seated class, looking like a strange nursery school in their loose white *gis*, studied the problem.

Janet looked grim. "Land on my butt, looks like," she conceded, after a moment's evaluation. I heard a couple of snorts of laughter.

"Lily, what would you do next, now that you're in control of the situation?" Marshall's faintly Asian face gave me no hint of the best answer.

"I'd keep going up on the ankle," I told him, "like so." I lifted Janet's right foot another inch, and the knee of her supporting left leg began to buckle.

Marshall nodded briefly. He faced the other class members. Like the rest of us, Marshall was barefoot and wearing his *gi*. Its snowy whiteness, broken only by the black belt and the fist patch on his chest, emphasized the ivory of his skin. "How could Janet have avoided this situation?" he asked the motley group sitting against the mirrored wall. "Or having gotten into it, how can she get out?"

Raphael Roundtree, the largest and darkest man in the class, said, "She should've drawn her kick back quicker." I let go of Janet, though Marshall hadn't told me to, because she was beginning to have trouble keeping her balance. Janet looked relieved to have both feet on the floor, and she nodded to me by way of saying thanks.

"She shouldn't have kicked at all," Becca Whitley rebutted.

"What should Janet have done instead?" Marshall asked her, a sweep of his hand inviting Becca to show us. She got up in one fluid movement. Becca often braided her hair for class—and she'd done so tonight—but she didn't lay off the makeup. Her toenails were bright scarlet, which for some reason struck me as improper for karate . . . though scarlet toenails didn't seem to bother Marshall, and it was his class.

Marshall Sedaka, our *sensei,* was also the owner of Body Time, where we were holding the class in the big aerobics room. I'd known Marshall for years. At one time, he'd been more to me than a friend. Now he straightened and moved closer to get a better view.

Janet moved away and Becca took her place, lifting and cocking her leg slowly so everyone could see what she meant to do.

"So," she said, her narrow face intent, "I kick, like so. . . ." Her foot began moving toward my abdomen, as Janet's had. "Then Lily takes a little hop back and her hand reaches for my ankle. That's what she did with Janet."

I obliged, imitating my movements of moments ago.

"But," continued Becca cheerfully, "that was a feint. I snap it back and aim it higher this time." Her leg floated back toward her, bent double at the knee, and lashed out again at my head. Becca was one of the few people in the class who could even attempt a head kick with any hope of success. "See," Becca pointed out, "she's leaning to reach my ankle, so her head's a little lower than usual."

I held still, with some effort, while Becca's foot with its bright nails flashed toward my face. Becca pulled the kick about an inch from my nose. I exhaled, I hoped silently. Becca winked at me.

"Good move, Becca," Marshall said. "But not an option open to many of the people in this class. Carlton, what would you do?"

Carlton was my next-door neighbor. He owned a little house almost identical to mine on Track Street, so if I stood facing my house, his would be on the right, and the Shakespeare Garden Apartments slightly uphill to my left. With his thick dark hair and large brown eyes, Carlton, single and self-supporting, was a real honeypot to Shakespeare's buzzing little hive of single women. Carlton went from one to the other, dating one for a month or two, then another; he wasn't as reckless as Deedra by a long shot, but he wasn't as careful as I was, either. In karate, Carlton was too slow and cautious, to his detriment. Maybe that caution, that deliberation, came from his being an accountant.

"I wouldn't kick at Lily at all," Carlton said frankly, and Janet and Raphael laughed. "I'm heavier than she is, and that's my only advantage with her. I'd try to strike her harder and hope that would take her out of the fight."

"Come try." Marshall returned to his spot against the wall.

With a marked reluctance, my neighbor scrambled to his feet and approached me slowly, while Becca folded gracefully to the floor with the rest of the students. I dropped into my fighting stance, knees slightly bent, one side turned toward Carlton.

"I'm supposed to stand and let him try to hit me?" I asked Marshall.

"No, give him some trouble," Marshall directed, so Carlton and I began circling each other. I moved in a sort of smooth, sideways glide that kept me evenly balanced. My hands were up, fisted and ready. Carlton *was* a lot taller and heavier than I was, so I kept reminding myself not to discount him as an opponent. What I didn't allow for was the macho factor and Carlton's inexperience. Carlton was determined to best me, and inexperienced enough to gauge his strike wrong.

He struck at my ribs, *seiken,* with his left fist, and I blocked him, my right forearm coming up under his striking arm to deflect it upward. I didn't propel his arm sideways enough—definitely my mistake—so instead of his punch landing in the air to my right, as I'd intended, his momentum carried him forward and his fist smacked my jaw.

The next thing I knew, I was down on the mat and Carlton was leaning over me, looking absolutely horror-struck.

"Dammit, Lily, say something!" he said frantically, and then Marshall shoved him aside and took his place.

He peered at my eyes, asked me several interesting questions about what parts of my body I could move and how many fingers I could see, and then said, "I think you're gonna be okay."

"Can I stand up?" I asked peevishly. I was deeply chagrined at having been knocked down by Carlton Cockroft, of all people. The rest of the class was crowding around me, but since Marshall had said I was in no danger, I swore I could see some suppressed grins.

"Here," Janet Shook said, her square little face both worried and amused. I gripped her outstretched hand and she braced her feet and pulled. With a little help from my own feet, I stood upright, and though everything looked funny for a second, I decided I was almost normal.

"Line up!" Marshall barked, and we took our places in line. I was sandwiched between Becca and Raphael.

"Kiotske!"

We put our heels together and stood to attention.

"Rei!"

We bowed.

"Class dismissed."

Still feeling a tad shaky, I walked carefully over to my little pile of belongings, pulled off my sparring pads, and stowed them in my gym bag. I slid my feet into my sandals, thankful I didn't have to bend over to tie sneakers.

Janet joined me as I walked out to my old car.

"Are you really feeling all right?" she asked quietly.

My first impulse was to snarl at her, but instead I admitted, "Not quite." She relaxed, as if she'd expected the snarl and was pleasantly surprised at the admission.

I fumbled with unlocking my car, but finally got it right.

Janet said, "I'm sorry about Deedra. I'm sorry you had to find her. It must have been awful."

I tilted my head in a brief nod. "I guess you and Deedra had known each other for a long time, both growing up here and all."

Janet nodded, her thick brown hair swinging against each cheek. She'd let it grow to chin length, and wore bangs. It became her. "Deedra was a little younger," she said, leaning against my car. I threw my gym bag in to land on the passenger's seat, and propped myself against the open door. It was a beautiful night, clear and just a little cool. We wouldn't have many more evenings like this; summer practically pounces on spring in southern Arkansas.

"I was a year ahead of her in school," Janet continued after a minute. "I went to Sunday school with her at First Methodist. That was before they formed Shakespeare Combined Church, and way before Miss Lacey's first husband died and she married Jerrell Knopp and began going to SCC. My mom is still real good friends with Miss Lacey."

"Was Deedra always . . . promiscuous?" I asked, since I seemed to be expected to keep the conversation going.

"No," Janet said. "Not always. It was her chin."

And I understood. Her severely recessive chin was the only feature that had kept Deedra from real prettiness, the flaw that had kept her from being homecoming queen, head cheerleader, most prized girl to date—everything. It was easy to imagine Deedra gradually coming to feel that if she couldn't achieve those things, she could be remarkable in another way.

"Wonder why her parents didn't do anything about it?" I asked. "Is there anything you can do about chins?"

"I don't know." Janet shrugged. "But I can tell you that Lacey has never believed in plastic surgery. She's real fundamentalist, you know. A great lady, but not a liberal bone in her body. That's why she took to Shakespeare Combined Church so well, when she married Jerrell and he wanted her to go to church with him."

A tap on the jaw seemed to have much the same effect on me as a glass or two of wine. I felt disinclined to move, oddly content to be standing in a parking lot having an idle conversation with another human being.

"Jerrell and Deedra didn't get along so well," I commented.

"No. Frankly, I've always wondered . . ." and Janet hesitated, her face compressing into an expression of both reluctance and distaste. "Well, I've always wondered if he ever visited Deedra . . . you know? Before Lacey's husband died, before Jerrell ever imagined being able to marry Lacey?"

"Ugh," I said. I turned this over in my mind for a minute. "Oh, *yuck.*"

"Yeah, me too." Our eyes met. We had matching expressions.

"I would think he would hate remembering that," Janet said, slowly and carefully. "I would think he'd hate wondering if Deedra would ever tell."

After a long, thoughtful moment, I replied, "Yes. I'd think he certainly would."

THREE

Lacey Knopp called me the next morning. I was about to leave for Joe C Prader's house when the phone rang. Hoping it was Jack, though the time difference made me fairly surely it wasn't, I said, "Yes?"

"Lily, I need you to help me," Lacey said. I hardly recognized her voice. She sounded like she'd been dragged over razor blades.

"How?"

"I need you to meet me at Deedra's tomorrow. I need help packing up the things in her apartment. Can you do that for me?"

I try to keep Wednesday mornings free for just such special projects. I wasn't more than a little surprised that Deedra's mother was in such a hurry to clear out Deedra's apartment. Many, many people react to grief with a furious flurry of activity. They figure if they don't hold still, it can't hit them.

"Yes, I can do that. What time?"

"Eight?"

"Sure." I hesitated. "I'm sorry," I said.

"Thank you." Lacey sounded shakier, suddenly. "I'll see you tomorrow."

I was so buried in thought that I took the wrong route to Mr. Prader's, and had to turn around and go back.

Joe Christopher Prader was as old as God but as mean as the devil. Called "Joe C" by all his family and cronies (those few still surviving), he'd been known for years for stalking around Shakespeare brandishing a cane at everyone who crossed his path, lamenting the passing of the better days, and bringing up old scandals at the most inopportune times.

Now Joe C's stalking-around days were pretty much done.

Some visits, I kind of enjoyed him. Others, I would have decked him gladly if he hadn't been so frail. More than once, I wondered if he was really as fragile as he seemed, or if maybe that show of frailty was a defense against just such impulses as mine.

Shakespeareans were inexplicably proud of having Joe C as a town character. His family was less thrilled. When his granddaughter Calla had hired me, she'd begged me to work for at least a month before I quit. By that time, she hoped, I would be over the shock of him.

"If we could get him to move out of that old house," Calla Prader had said despairingly. "If we could get him into Shakespeare Manor . . . or if we could get him to agree to live-in help!"

Joe C was definitely not in the business of making life easier for anyone but himself, and that only when it suited him.

But I'd lasted my month, and was now into my third.

Joe C was up and dressed by the time I knocked on his door. He adamantly refused to let me have a key, so every week I had to wait for him to shuffle from his bedroom to the front door, which I tried to bear philosophically. After all, keeping his keys to himself was his right, and one I understood.

But I was sure he wouldn't give me a key simply out of meanness, rather than from principle. I'd noticed he came to the door especially slowly when the weather was bad, and I suspected he relished the idea of keeping me out in the rain or cold; anyway, keeping me at the mercy of Joe C Prader, all-powerful doorkeeper.

This morning he swung the door open after only a short delay. "Well, here you are, then," he said, amazed and disgusted by my persistence in arriving on time for my job.

"Here I am," I agreed. I tried not to sigh too loudly when he turned to go ahead of me to his bedroom, where I usually started by stripping the bed. Joe C always had to lead the way, and he always went very, very slowly. But the man was a nonagenarian: What could I say? I looked around me at the remains of the grand house as I followed the old man. The Prader House, the only remaining home on one of the main commercial streets of Shakespeare, was a showplace that had seen better days. Built about 1890, the house had high ceilings, beautiful woodwork, restored but cranky plumbing, and an electrical system that had seen better decades. The upstairs, with its four bedrooms and huge bathroom, was closed off now, though Calla had told me that she cleaned it about twice a year. Joe C wasn't fit to go up stairs anymore.

"I'm all stopped up this week." Joe C opened the conversation, which would not let up until I left the house. He lowered himself into the old red velvet chair in a corner of the large back bedroom.

"Allergies?" I said absently, stripping the bedding off the four-poster and pitching it into the hall, where I'd gather it up and take it to the washer. I shook out the bedspread and draped it over the footboard.

"Naw, I reckon I ate too much cheese. You know, it binds you."

I exhaled slowly, calmly, as I stepped out into the hall to open the linen cupboard.

"Did you get Calla to get you some prunes?"

He cackled. I was one ahead of him. "Yes, missy, I surely did, and ate them all. Today's the day."

I wasn't in the best mood to put up with Joe C this morning. The charm of this particular town character was lost on me; maybe the sightseers the Chamber of Commerce was trying to attract would appreciate hearing colorful stories about Joe C's intestines. I couldn't imagine why any tourist would want to come to Shakespeare, since its only possible attraction would have been antebellum homes—if they hadn't been burned to the ground in the Late Unpleasantness, as Joe C's best friend, China Belle Lipscott, called the Civil War. So all Shakespeare could boast was, "Yes, we're old, but we have nothing to show for it."

Maybe Joe C could be propped on a bench on the square to amuse any soul who happened by. He could give a daily report on the state of his bowels.

"China Belle's daughter is dropping her off in a few

minutes," Joe C informed me. "Is my tie crooked?"

I straightened from putting on the fitted sheet. I suspected he'd been eyeing my ass. "You're okay," I said unenthusiastically.

"China Belle's quite a gal," he said, trying to leer.

"You creep," I said. "Mrs. Lipscott is a perfectly nice woman who wouldn't go to bed with you if you owned the last mattress on earth. You stop talking dirty."

"Oooh," he said, in mock fear. "Bully the old man, why dontcha. Come on, darlin', make old Joe C feel good again."

That did it.

"Listen to me," I said intently, squatting before him. He put his cane between us, I noticed, so he hadn't completely ruled out the fact that I might retaliate.

Good.

"You will not tell me about your body functions. Unless you're dripping blood, I don't care. You will not make sexual remarks."

"Or what? You're going to hit me, a man in his nineties who walks with a cane?"

"Don't rule it out. Disgusting is disgusting."

He eyed me malevolently. His brown eyes were almost hidden in the folds of skin that drooped all over him. "Calla wouldn't pay you, you go to hit me," he said in defiance.

"It'd be worth losing the pay."

He glared at me, resenting like hell his being old and powerless. I didn't blame him for that. I might feel exactly the same way if I reach his age. But there are some things I just won't put up with.

39

"Oh, all right," he conceded. He looked into a corner of the room, not at me, and I rose and went back to making up the bed.

"You knew that gal that got killed, that Deedra?"

"Yes."

"She was my great-granddaughter. She as loose as they say?"

"Yes," I said, answering the second part of the question before the first had registered. Then I glared at him, shocked and angry.

"When I was a boy, it was Fannie Dooley," Joe C said reminiscently, one gnarled hand rising to pat what was left of his hair. He was elaborately ignoring my anger. I'd seen a picture of Joe C when he was in his twenties: he'd had thick black hair, parted in the middle, and a straight, athletic body. He'd had a mouthful of healthy, if not straight, teeth. He'd started up a hardware store, and his sons had worked there with him until Joe Jr. had died early in World War II. After that, Joe C and his second son, Christopher, had kept Prader Hardware going for many more years. Joe C Prader had been a hard worker and man of consequence in Shakespeare. It must be his comparative helplessness that had made him so perverse and aggravating.

"Fannie Dooley?" I prompted. I was *not* going to gratify him by expressing my shock.

"Fannie was the town bad girl," he explained. "There's always one, isn't there? The girl from a good family, the kind that likes to do it, don't get paid?"

"Is there always one?"

"I think every small town's got one or two," Joe C

40

observed. "Course it's bad when it's your own flesh and blood."

"I guess so." At my high school, a million years ago, it'd been Teresa Black. She'd moved to Little Rock and married four times since then. "Deedra was your great-granddaughter?" I asked, surprised I'd never realized the connection.

"Sure was, darlin'. Every time she came around to see me, she was the picture of sweetness. I don't believe I ever would have guessed."

"You're awful," I said dispassionately. "Someone's going to push you off your porch or beat you over the head."

"They's always going to be bad girls," he said, almost genially. "Else, how's the good girls going to know they're good?"

I couldn't decide if that was really profound or just stupid. I shrugged and turned my back on the awful man, who told my back that he was going to get gussied up for his girlfriend.

By the time I'd worked my way through the ground floor of the old house, whose floors were none too level, Joe C and China Belle Lipscott were ensconced on the front porch in fairly comfortable padded wicker chairs, each with a glass of lemonade close to hand. They were having a round of "What Is This World Coming To?" based on Deedra's murder. There may have been a town bad girl when they were growing up, but there'd also been plenty to eat for everyone, everyone had known their place, prices had been cheap, and almost no one had been murdered. Maybe the occasional black man had been hung without benefit of jury, maybe the occasional unwed

41

mother had died from a botched abortion, and just possibly there'd been a round of lawlessness when oil had been discovered . . . but Joe C and China Belle chose to remember their childhood as perfect.

I found evidence (a filtered butt) that Joe C had once again been smoking. One of my little jobs was to tell Calla if I found traces of cigarettes, because Joe C had almost set the house afire once or twice by falling asleep with a cigarette in his hands. The second time that had happened, he'd been unconscious and his mattress smoldering when Calla had happened to drop by. Who could be smuggling the old man cigarettes? Someone who wanted him to enjoy one of his last pleasures, or someone who wanted him to die faster? I extricated the coffee mug he'd used as an ashtray from the depths of his closet and took it to the kitchen to wash.

I wondered if the old house was insured for much. Its location alone made it valuable, even if the structure itself was about to fall down around Joe C's ears. There were businesses now in the old homes on either side of the property, though the thick growth around the old place made them largely invisible from the front or back porch. The increased traffic due to the businesses (an antique store in one old home and a ladies' dress shop in the other) gratified Joe C no end, since he still knew everyone in town and related some nasty story about almost every person who drove by.

As I was putting my cleaning items away, Calla came in. She often timed her appearance so she'd arrive just as I was leaving, probably so she could check the job I'd done and vent her misery a little. Perhaps Calla thought that if she didn't keep an eye on me, I'd slack up on the job, since Joe C was certainly no critic of my work (unless he couldn't think of another way to rile me). Calla was a horse of a different color. Overworked (at least according to her) at her office job in the local mattress-manufacturing plant, perpetually harried, Calla was determined no one should cheat her any more than she'd already been cheated. She must have been a teenager once, must have laughed and dated boys, but it was hard to believe this pale, dark-haired woman had ever been anything but middle-aged and worried.

"How is he today?" she asked me in a low voice.

Since she'd passed her grandfather on her way in, and he was loudly in fine form, I didn't respond. "He's been smoking again," I said reluctantly, since I felt like a spy for telling on Joe C. At the same time, I didn't want him to burn up.

"Lily, who could be bringing him cigarettes?" Calla slapped the counter with a thin white hand. "I've asked and asked, and no one will admit it. And yet, for someone who can't go to the store himself, he seems to have unlimited access to the things he's not supposed to have!"

"Who visits him?"

"Well, it's a complicated family." Though it didn't seem complicated to me, as Calla began to explain it. I knew already that Joe C had had three children. The first was Joe Jr., who had died childless during World War II. The second boy, Christopher, had been the father of Calla, Walker, and Lacey. These three were the only surviving grandchildren of Joe C. Calla had never married. Walker, now living in North Carolina, had three teenage children, and Lacey had Deedra during her first marriage.

Calla's aunt (Joe C's third child), Jessie Lee Prader,

43

had married Albert Albee. Jessie Lee and Albert had had two children, Alice (who'd married a James Whitley from Texas, moved there with him and had two children by him) and Pardon, who had been the owner of the Shakespeare Garden Apartments. When Pardon had died, he'd left the apartments to Alice Albee Whitley's children, Becca and Anthony, since the widowed Alice had herself died of cancer two years before.

The final complication was Joe C's sister, Arnita, who was much younger than Joe C. In the way of those times, the two babies their mother had had between them had died at birth or in infancy. Arnita married Howell Winthrop and they became the parents of Howell Winthrop, Jr., my former employer. Therefore, Joe C's sister was the grandmother of my young friend Bobo Winthrop and his brother, Howell III, and his sister, Amber Jean.

"So you, Becca Whitley and her brother, and the Winthrops are all related," I concluded. Since I was cleaning the kitchen counter, I had been gainfully employed while listening to this long and fairly boring discourse.

Calla nodded. "I was so glad when Becca moved here. I was crazy about Alice, and I hadn't gotten to see her in so many years." Calla looked wistful, but her mood changed abruptly. "Though you see who owns a whole building, who ended up in the mansion, and who's sitting in the house that's about to be zoned commercial," she said sourly. Becca had the rent income, the Winthrops were wealthy from the lumber yard, the sporting goods store, and oil, while Calla's little house was sandwiched between an insurance office and small engine repair service.

There was no response to that. I was mostly indifferent to Calla, but I felt sorry for her some days. Other days, the resentment that was a cornerstone of her character grated at me, made me ornery.

"So, they all come around," she said, staring out the kitchen window, the steam from her cup of fresh coffee rising in front of her face in a sinister way. I realized for the first time that the day had become overcast, that the darkness was reaching into the room. Like lawn furniture, Joe C and China Belle had to be brought in before they blew away or got wet.

"Great grandchildren—Becca Whitley, all painted up; Deedra, in her slutty dresses . . . Joe C just loved that. And the great-nieces and -nephews—Howell III, asking can he help by mowing the yard . . . like he'd ever mowed his own yard in his life."

I hadn't realized Calla was quite this bitter. I turned around to look at the older woman, who almost seemed to be in a spell. I needed to go get the old people in, or else rouse Calla to do it. Thunder rumbled far away, and Calla's dark eyes scanned the sky outside, looking for the rain.

Finally she slid her gaze toward me, cold and remote.

"You can go," she said, as distant as if I'd tried to claim relationship to Joe C myself.

I gathered my paraphernalia and left without another word, leaving Calla to handle the business of relocating her grandfather and his girlfriend all by herself.

I wondered if Calla was glad of Deedra's death. Now there was one less person to come by, one less painted woman to titillate the old man and rob Calla of her possible inheritance.

FOUR

The sheriff was talking to Lacey Dean Knopp. Lacey, barely into her fifties, was a lovely blond woman with such an innocent face that almost everyone instantly wanted to give her his or her best manners, most conscientious opinion, hardest try. When I'd first met Lacey, the day she'd hired me to clean Deedra's apartment, that innocence had irritated me violently. But now, years later, I pitied Lacey all the more since she'd had farther to come to meet her grief.

The sheriff looked as though she'd slept only an hour or so for two nights in a row. Oh, her uniform was crisp and clean, her shoes were shiny, but her face had that crumpled, dusty look of sheets left too quick. I wondered how her brother Marlon was looking. If Marta Schuster had been thinking clearly, she'd deposited the grief-stricken young man away from public scrutiny.

"We're through in there," she was telling Lacey, who nodded numbly in response. Marta gave me the thousand-yard stare when I leaned against the wall, waiting for Lacey to give me the word to enter.

"Lily Bard," Marta said.

"Sheriff."

"You're here for what reason?" Marta asked, her eyebrows going up. Her expression, as I perceived it, was disdainful.

"I asked Lily," Lacey said. Her hands were gripping each other, and as I watched, Lacey drove the nails of her right hand into the skin on the back of her left hand. "Lily's going to help me clean out my daughter's apartment," Lacey went on. Her voice was dull and lifeless.

"Oh, she is," the sheriff said, as though that was somehow significant.

I waited for her to move, and when she got tired of pondering, she stepped aside to let us in. But as I passed her, she tapped my shoulder. While Lacey stood stock still in the living room, I hung back and looked at the sheriff inquiringly.

She peered past me to make sure Lacey was not listening. Then she leaned uncomfortably close and said, "Clean out the box under the bed and the bottom drawer of the chest of drawers in the second bedroom."

I understood after a second, and nodded.

Lacey hadn't registered any of this. As I closed the apartment door behind me, I saw that Lacey was staring around her as though she'd never seen her daughter's place before.

She caught my eyes. "I never came up here much," she said ruefully. "I was so used to my house being 'home,' that's where I always felt Deedra belonged. I guess a mother always thinks her child is just playing at being a grown-up."

I'd never felt so sorry for anyone. But feeling sorry for Lacey wasn't going to help her. She had plenty of pity available, if she wanted it. What she needed was practical help.

"Where did you want to start?" I asked. I could hardly march into the bedrooms to start looking for whatever Marta Schuster had wanted me to remove.

"Jerrell carried these up earlier," she said, pointing at the pile of broken-down boxes and two rolls of trash bags. Then she stood silently again.

"Do you want to keep any of Deedra's things?" I asked, trying to prod her into giving me directions. "For yourself?"

Lacey forced herself to answer. "Some of the jewelry, maybe," she said, in a fairly steady voice. "None of the clothes; she wore a size smaller than I do." Plus, Lacey Knopp wouldn't be caught dead in her daughter's just-this-side-of-tarty clothes. "Could you use any of them?"

I took a moment so I wouldn't look like I was rejecting the offer without thinking it over. "No, I'm too broad in the shoulders," I said, which was on a par with Lacey claiming the clothes would be a size small. Then I thought of my bank account and I remembered I needed a winter coat. "If there's a coat or a jacket that fits me, maybe I'd need that," I said reluctantly, and Lacey looked almost grateful. "So, where do you want the rest of the clothes to go?"

"SCC has a clothes closet for the needy," Lacey said. "I should take them there." Shakespeare Combined

Church was right down the street from the apartment building. It was the busiest church in Shakespeare, at the moment, having just added a new Sunday-school wing.

"Won't that bother you?"

"Seeing some poor woman go around in Deedra's old clothes?" She hesitated. "No, I know Deedra would have wanted to help others."

I was trying to remember someone Deedra had helped (other than by relieving sexual tension) during her life when Lacey added, "All the kitchen things can go to the community relief fund. SCC doesn't keep anything but clothes." The town of Shakespeare kept a few rooms at the old community center filled with odds and ends cleaned out from people's cabinets and attics: pots and pans, dishes, sheets, blankets, utensils. The purpose of this accumulation was to re-equip families who had met with a disaster. In our part of the country, "disasters" generally translate as fires or tornadoes.

Again Lacey stood in silence for a few long moments.

"Where would you like me to begin?" I said as gently as I could.

"Her clothes, please. That would be hardest for me." And Lacey turned and went into the kitchen with one of the boxes.

I admired her courage.

I got a box of my own, reassembled it, and went into the larger bedroom.

Everything had been searched, of course. I guess the police always hope to find a piece of paper with *Am meeting Joe Doe at 8:00. If evil befalls me, he is the guilty one* written on it. But I was pretty sure no one had found such a note, and I didn't find it either, though I conscientiously checked the pockets of each garment and the inside of every shoe as I packed boxes.

When I was sure Lacey was busy in the kitchen, I reached under Deedra's bed and slid out a box she'd stuffed under there. I'd only cleared under the bed a couple of times before, when Deedra (actually Lacey) had paid for a spring-cleaning. Then, Deedra had had plenty of warning to conceal this carved wooden box with its tight-fitting lid. I lifted it a little to look inside. After a long, comprehensive stare at the contents I slammed it shut and wondered where I could hide it from Lacey.

It had been years since I'd thought of myself as naive. But I discovered that not only could I still be shocked, but also I could say that whole areas of my life were unsophisticated.

I peeked again.

A couple of the sex toys in the box were easily identifiable, even to someone like me who'd never seen the like. But one or two baffled me. I knew their function was something I'd puzzle over in odd moments for some time to come, and the idea didn't make me happy. As I pushed the box back under the edge of the bedspread till I could think of a way to get it out of the apartment surreptitiously, I found myself wondering if Jack had ever used such items. I was embarrassed at the thought of asking him, to my astonishment. I hadn't realized there was anything we could say or do between us that would be embarrassing. Interesting.

I glanced out into the hall before I slipped into the guest bedroom. I opened the drawer the sheriff had designated, and discovered it was full of odds and ends like handcuffs, stained silk scarves, heavy cord . . . and movies.

"Oh, man," I muttered as the titles registered. I could feel my face grow hot with shame. How could she have made herself so vulnerable? How could she have put herself at someone's mercy this way? It seemed to me that only a woman who'd never experienced sexual violence would think the imitation of it a turn-on. Maybe I was being naive about that, too, I thought gloomily.

I stuffed all the paraphernalia into a garbage bag, and deposited it under the bed with the carved box. Then I started packing clothes swiftly to make up for the lost time.

I resumed my task by opening the top drawer of Deedra's lingerie chest. I wondered how pleased the women's group at Shakespeare Combined Church would be to get some of Deedra's exotic play clothes. Would the deserving poor be thrilled with a leopard-print thong and matching baby-doll nightie?

Soon I moved to the chest of drawers and more mundane items. As I folded everything neatly, I tried to keep all the categories together: slacks, spring dresses, T-shirts, shorts. I assumed Deedra had moved her out-of-season clothes to the closet of the second bedroom. That was where the jackets would be.

I was right. The second closet was just as packed as the first, but with fall and winter clothes. Most of her suits and dresses would be categorized as Professional—Slut Subsection. Deedra had loved dressing up for work. She'd liked her job, too; since she'd completed two mediocre years at junior college, Deedra had been a clerk in the county clerk's office. In Arkansas, the office of county clerk is an elected two-year position, quite often held by a woman. In Shakespeare's county, Hartsfield, a man,

Choke Anson, had won the last election. My friend Claude Friedrich, the chief of police, thought Choke intended to use the office as an entrance to county politics, and thence to the state arena.

I was probably the least political person in Hartsfield County. In Arkansas, politics are a cross between a tabloid concoction and a brawl. Politicians in Arkansas are not afraid to be colorful, and they love to be folksy. Though my conscience would not permit to me to skip voting, I often voted for the lesser of two evils. This past election, Choke Anson had been the lesser. I knew his opponent, Mary Elwood, having observed her at the SCC while I served the board meeting there. Mary Elwood was a stupid, ultraconservative homophobe who believed with absolute sincerity that she knew the will of God. She further believed that people who disagreed with her were not only wrong, but also evil. I'd figured Choke Anson simply couldn't be as bad. Now I wondered how Deedra had managed with a male superior.

"Did you pick a jacket?"

"What?" I was so startled I jumped.

Lacey brought another box into the room. "Sorry, I didn't mean to scare you," she said wearily. "I was just hoping you'd found a jacket you could use. Deedra thought so highly of you, I know she'd like you to have whatever you could use."

It was news to me that Deedra'd thought of me at all, much less that she'd had any particular regard for me. I would have been interested to hear that conversation, if it had ever taken place.

There was a forest-green thigh-length coat with a zip-out lining that would be very useful, and there was a leather jacket that I admired. The other coats and jackets were too fancy, or impractical, or looked too narrow in the shoulders. I didn't remember seeing Deedra wearing either of the ones I liked, so maybe they wouldn't be such reminders to her mother.

"These?" I asked, holding them up.

"Anything you want," Lacey said, not even turning to look at my choices. I realized that she didn't want to know, didn't want to mark the clothes so when she saw me she wouldn't think of Deedra. I folded the garments and went back into Deedra's larger bedroom. There, I quickly placed the carved box into a reassembled carton, and put the plastic bag of "toys" in with it. I laid the two jackets on top, covering up the contraband. I wrote *Lily* on the top in Magic Marker, hoping that even if Lacey wondered why I'd put the jackets in a box instead of carrying them out over my arm, she'd be too preoccupied to ask.

We worked all morning, Lacey and I. Twice, Lacey went into the bathroom abruptly and I could hear her crying through the door. Since the apartment was so quiet, I had time to wonder why some friend of Lacey's wasn't helping her with this homely task. Surely this was the time when family and friends stepped in.

Then I noticed that Lacey was staring at a picture she'd pulled out of a drawer in the kitchen. I was in there only because the dust in the closet had made me thirsty.

Though I couldn't see the picture myself, Lacey's reaction told me what it was. I saw her expression of confusion, and then her cheeks turned red as she held it closer to her eyes as if she disbelieved what she was seeing. She chucked it in a trash bag with unnecessary force. Maybe,

I thought, Lacey had had an inkling she would be finding items like this, and maybe she'd decided she couldn't risk any of her friends she saw socially having a peek at her daughter's playthings. Maybe Lacey was not quite as oblivious as she seemed.

I was glad I'd followed the sheriff's hints, glad I was the one to dispose of the items now in the box marked with my name. Lacey might happen upon a thing or two I'd missed, but there wasn't any point in grinding her face in her daughter's misbehavior.

I began to think better of Marta Schuster. She'd gotten rid of most of the pictures, so now they wouldn't be added to the local lore; and she'd warned me about the other stuff, so I'd had a chance to get it out of sight before Lacey had had to look at it. We couldn't block her from all knowledge, but we could dispose of a lot of the more graphic evidence.

By noon, when I had to go, we'd accomplished a lot. I'd emptied the closet and the chests in the larger bedroom, and made a beginning on the closet in the spare bedroom. Lacey had packed most of the kitchen items and some of the towels in the bathroom. I'd made five or six trips to the Dumpster in the parking lot.

A life couldn't be dismantled so quickly, but we'd made quite a start on Deedra's.

As I picked up the labeled box and my purse, Lacey asked me when I had more time to spare, and I realized that now I had Friday mornings open, since my client was dead.

"I can meet you here on Friday," I said. "Early as you want."

"That would be great. Eight o'clock too early?"

55

I shook my head.

"I'll see you then," Lacey said, "and maybe before Friday I can have Jerrell come over with his truck and get some of these boxes delivered, so we'll have more room to work."

She sounded detached, but I knew that couldn't be true. Numb was probably more accurate.

"Excuse me," I began, and then I hesitated. "When will the funeral be?"

"We're hoping to get her back here in time for a funeral on Saturday," Lacey said.

As I carried the box down the stairs, I returned to a familiar worry. I'd have to get another regular client for Friday mornings. I'd had Deedra and the Winthrops on Friday; then the Winthrops had dropped me, and now Deedra was dead. My financial future was looking grimmer by the week.

I was supposed to meet my friend Carrie Thrush at her office; Carrie had said she'd bring a bag lunch for us both. I got in my car, stowing the box in the backseat. Minutes later, I glanced at my watch to find I was running a little late, because I had to find a business Dumpster on the other side of Shakespeare, one that wasn't too visible, and deposit the box of sex paraphernalia after removing the two jackets. I was certain no one saw me. By the time I turned in to Carrie's office, I assumed she'd be in her office, fussing over food growing cold.

But when I pulled down the small driveway marked STAFF PARKING ONLY, Carrie was standing in the little graveled lot behind her clinic, where she and her nurses parked their cars.

"Want to go somewhere with me?" Carrie's smile was stiff and self-conscious. She was wearing white, but it wasn't her lab coat, I realized after a second's scrutiny. She was wearing a white dress with a lacy white collar. I could feel my eyebrows draw together in a frown.

I didn't remember ever seeing Carrie in a dress, except at a funeral. Or a wedding.

"What?" I asked sharply.

"Go with me to the courthouse?"

"For?"

Her face scrunched up, causing her glasses to slide down her small nose.

Carrie had on makeup. And her hair wasn't pulled back behind her ears, as she usually wore it at work. It swung forward in shining brown wings.

"For?" I asked more insistently.

"Well . . . Claude and I are going to get married today."

"At the courthouse?" I tried not to sound astonished, but she flushed.

"We have to do it before we lose our courage," she said in a rush. "We're both set in our ways, we both have everything we could need to start a household, and we both want to have just a couple of good friends at the ceremony. The marriage license list'll be out in the paper tomorrow and then everyone will know." The legal notices always appeared in the local paper on Thursday afternoon.

"But . . ." I looked down at my working clothes, not exactly pristine after getting into closets and under beds at Deedra's.

"If you want to run home, we have a few minutes,"

she said, glancing down at her watch. "Not that I care what you wear, but if I know you, it'll bother you the whole time."

"Yes, not being clean at a wedding does bother me," I said shortly. "Get in the car."

I couldn't say why I felt a little angry, but I did. Maybe it was the surprise of it (I'm not fond of surprises) or maybe it was the switch in moods required of me: from death to marriage in a single day. I had become sure Claude Friedrich and Dr. Carrie Thrush would get married, and I'd become sure it was a good idea. The difference in ages was substantial; Claude was probably forty-eight or so, and Carrie was about thirty-two. But I was confident their marriage would work, and I hadn't regretted turning down a chance to try intimacy with Claude myself. So why was I upset? I owed it to Carrie to be happy.

I made myself smile as Carrie ran on and on about why they'd made their decision, how her parents were going to take it, how soon they could get Claude's things moved into her small house.

"What about a honeymoon?" I asked, as I turned the key in the lock of my own little house, Carrie practically on my heels.

"That's going to have to wait for a month," Carrie said. "We'll take a long weekend starting today, from now until Monday night, but we're not going far. And Claude has to take his beeper with him."

While Carrie alternated staring in the mirror and pacing the floor, I stripped off my cleaning clothes and pulled out my good black suit. No. Couldn't wear black to a wedding. I grasped the hanger holding my sleeveless white dress. No, couldn't wear white either.

But after a second's consideration, I realized I had to. I camouflaged it with my black jacket and a black belt, and I tucked a bright blue scarf into the neckline. I pulled up my thigh-highs, slid on my good black shoes, and replaced Carrie in front of the bathroom mirror to repowder and to fluff my short curly hair.

"I would have given you a wedding shower," I said sourly, and met Carrie's eyes. After a little pause, we both began laughing, because that seemed such an unlikely scenario to both of us.

"Are you ready? You look pretty," Carrie said, giving me a careful once-over.

"You too," I said honestly. With her short-sleeved white dress, she was wearing brown pumps and carrying a brown purse. She looked fine, but not exactly festive. We got back into my car, and as we passed a florist, I pulled in to the curb.

"What?" Carrie asked anxiously. "We're late."

"Hold on a minute," I said, and ran into the shop.

"I need a corsage," I told the old woman that came to help me.

"An orchid?" she asked. "Or some nice carnations?"

"Not carnations," I told her. "An orchid, with white net and a colored ribbon."

This admirable woman didn't ask questions, she just went to work. In less than ten minutes, I was handing Carrie the orchid, netted in white and beribboned in green, and she tearfully pinned it to her dress.

"Now you really look like a bride," I said, and the knot inside me eased.

"I wish Jack were here," Carrie said politely, though she hadn't really had much of a chance to know him. "Claude and I would have enjoyed him being with us."

"He's still in California," I told her. "I don't know when he'll be back."

"I hope you two..." but Carrie didn't finish that thought, and I was grateful.

The courthouse, which occupies a whole block downtown, is an old one, but recently renovated. Claude was waiting on the wheelchair ramp.

"He's wearing a suit," I said, amazed almost beyond speech. I'd never seen Claude in anything but his uniform or blue jeans.

"Doesn't he look handsome?" Carrie's cheeks, normally on the sallow end of the spectrum, took on a becoming rose tint. In fact, she looked more twenty-five than thirty-two.

"Yes," I said gently. "He looks wonderful."

Claude's brother, Charles, was with him, looking more uncomfortable than Claude did. Charles was more at home in overalls and a welder's cap than a suit. Shy and solitary by nature, Charles managed to make himself almost invisible even in this small town. I thought I could count on my fingers the number of times I'd seen Charles in the years I'd lived in Shakespeare.

He'd really made an effort today.

When Claude saw Carrie coming up the sidewalk, his face changed. I watched the hardness seep out of it, replaced by something more. He took her hand, and brought his other hand from behind him to present her with a bouquet.

"Oh, Claude," she said, overcome with pleasure. "You thought of this."

Good. Much better than my corsage. Now Carrie looked truly bridelike.

"Claude, Charles," I said, by way of greeting.

"Lily, thanks for coming. Let's go do it."

If Claude had been any more nervous he would've made a hole in the sidewalk.

I spied Judge Hitchcock peering out of the door.

"Judge is waiting," I said, and Claude and Carrie looked at each other, heaved a simultaneous sigh, and started toward the courthouse door. Charles and I were right behind.

After the brief ceremony, Claude and Carrie had eyes only for each other, though Carrie hugged Charles and me, and Claude shook our hands. He offered to buy us lunch, but with one voice we turned him down. Charles wanted to crawl back in his cave, wherever it was, and I was not in a festive mood after my morning's work, though I was making an effort to be cheerful for my friends' sakes.

Charles and I were glad to part, and as Carrie and her new husband drove away to their weekend prehoneymoon, I went back to my house, despising myself for my nasty mood, which I hoped I'd hidden well enough. Changing back into my working clothes, hanging my good outfit in the closet, and grabbing a piece of fruit for lunch, I was restless from the dark feeling inside me. As always, it translated into a need for action. It would have been a good day for me to be mugged, because I would have enjoyed hurting someone.

While I cleaned the tiny house of the very old Mrs.

Jepperson, while the round black woman who "sat with" Mrs. Jepperson every day did her best to catch me stealing something, I carried that core of anger within me, burning and painful.

It took me an hour to identify my anger as loneliness. It had been a long time since I'd felt lonely; I'm a person who enjoys being alone, and the past few years had afforded me plenty of that. For a long time, I hadn't made friends; I hadn't taken lovers. But this year had seen so many changes in me, and unfortunately, side by side with the willingness to have friends traveled the capacity for loneliness. I sighed as I put Mrs. Jepperson's stained sheets in the washer to soak in bleach.

I was just plain old feeling sorry for myself. Even though I knew that, I didn't seem to be able to quench that resentful smoldering inside me.

I went to my next job, and then home, without being able to find a thought to still my inner restlessness. Jack, whose timing was often off, chose that moment to call me.

Every now and then Jack told me all about a case he was working on. But sometimes, especially in a case involving financial transactions and large sums of money, he kept his mouth shut, and this was one of those times. He missed me very much, he said. And I believed him. But I had unworthy thoughts, ideas that dismayed me; not their content, exactly, but the fact that *I* was having them. California, the home of tanned young hardbodies, I thought; Jack, the most passionate man I'd ever met, was in California. I wasn't jealous of a woman, but a *state*.

Not surprisingly, the conversation didn't go well. I was at my most clipped and inaccessible; Jack was frustrated and angry that I wasn't happier he'd called right in the middle of his busy day. I knew I was being impossible, without seeming to be able to stop it, and I believe he knew the same.

We needed to be together more. After we'd hung up, just barely managing not to snarl at each other, I made myself face the facts. One weekend every now and then wasn't enough. It took us hours to get re-accustomed to ourselves as a couple, together. After that we had a wonderful time, but then we had to go through the detachment process when Jack returned to Little Rock. His hours were unpredictable. My hours were generally regular. Only by living in the same town were we likely to see each other consistently enough to establish our relationship.

Your own life is plenty hard without complicating it with that of another. For a moment I wondered if we should stop trying. The idea was so painful that I had to admit to myself, all over again, that Jack was necessary to me.

I didn't want to call him back when I was so fraught. I couldn't predict what he would say, either. So what I ended up doing that evening was going into the empty guest bedroom and kicking the hell out of my punching bag.

FIVE

Thursday was biceps day in my personal schedule. Bicep curls may look impressive, but they're not my favorite exercise. And they're hard to do correctly. Most people swing the dumbbells up. Of course, the more swing you put in it, the less you're working your biceps. I've noticed that in every movie scene set in a gym, the characters are either doing bicep curls or bench presses. Usually the guy doing bicep curls is a jerk.

Just as I put the twenty-five-pound barbells back on the weight rack, Bobo Winthrop walked in with a girl. Bobo, though maybe twelve years younger than me, was my friend. I was glad to see him, and glad to see the girl accompanying him; for the past couple of years, even after all the trouble I'd had with his family, Bobo had been convinced that I was the woman for him. Now that Bobo divided his time between college in nearby Montrose and visits home to check on his ailing grandmother, visit his family, and do his laundry, I seldom got to visit with him. I realized I'd missed him, and that made me wary.

As I watched Bobo start working his way around the room, shaking hands and patting backs, I moved from free weights to the preacher bench. The short young woman in tow behind him kept smiling as Bobo, shoving his floppy blond hair out of his eyes, introduced her to the motley crew who inhabited the gym at this early hour. She had a good, easy, meet-and-greet style.

The early-morning people at Body Time ranged from Brian Gruber, an executive at a local mattress-manufacturing plant, to Jerri Sizemore, whose claim to fame was that she'd been married four times. As I put weights on the short curl bar at the preacher bench, I marked Bobo's progress with a touch of amusement. In his golden wake, he left smiles and some infusion of joie de vive.

What did it feel like, I wondered, to be almost universally known and liked, to be attractive to almost everyone, to have the backing of a strong and influential family?

With a shock like a dash of ice water, it occurred to me that I had once been like that, when I'd been about Bobo's age: before I'd gone off to live in Memphis, before the media-saturated nightmare of my abduction and rape. I shook my head. Though I knew it was true, I found it was almost impossible to believe I had ever been that comfortable. Bobo had had some hard times himself, at least in the past year, yet his long look into darkness had only made his radiance stand out with greater relief.

I'd finished my first set with the curl bar and returned it to its rests by the time Bobo worked his way around to me.

"Lily!" His voice was full of pride. Was he showing

me off to the girl, or the girl to me? His hand on my shoulder was warm and dry. "This is Toni Holbrook," he said. "Toni, this is my friend Lily Bard." The gaze of his dark blue eyes flicked back and forth between us.

I waited for my name to ring a bell with this girl—for the horrified fascination to creep into her gaze—but she was so young I guess she didn't remember the months when my name was in every newspaper. I relaxed and held out my hand to her. She stuck her fingers up against my palm instead of grasping my hand firmly. Almost always, the offenders who shake hands in this wishy-washy way are women. It felt like getting a handful of cannelloni.

"I'm so pleased to finally meet you," she said with a sincere smile that made my teeth hurt. "Bobo talks about you all the time."

I flashed a glance at him. "I used to clean for Bobo's mother," I said, to put a different perspective on the conversation. I'll give her this, she didn't flinch.

"What you want on there, Lily?" Bobo asked. He waited at the disc rack.

"Another set of dimes," I told him. He slid off two ten-pound discs, put one on each end of the bar, and then added clips to secure them. We were comfortable working with weights together; Bobo's first job had been here at the gym, and he'd spotted for me many a time. This morning, he took his position at the front of the bar and I straddled the seat, leaning over the padded rest, the backs of my hands toward the floor so I could grasp the bar to curl up. I nodded when I was ready, and he helped me lift the bar the first couple of inches. Then he let go, and I brought it up myself, squeezing until the bar touched my chin. I finished my ten reps without too much trouble, but

I was glad when Bobo helped me ease the bar down into the rack.

"Toni, are you here for the rest of the week?" I asked, making an effort to be polite for Bobo's sake. He slid the clips off, raising his blond eyebrows interrogatively. "Dime again," I said, and together we prepared the bar.

"Yes, we'll go back to Montrose on Sunday afternoon," Toni said, with equal politeness and a tiny, clear emphasis on the *we*. Her smooth black hair was cut just below chin-length, and looked as if it always stayed brushed. It swung in a lively dance when she moved her head. She had a sweet mouth and almond-shaped brown eyes. "I'm from DeQueen," she added, when her first sentence hung in the air for a second or two. I found I didn't care.

I nodded to show I was ready, and Bobo gave me a little boost to get the bar off the stand. With a lot more difficulty, I completed another set, making sure to breathe out as I lifted, in when I lowered. My muscles began to tremble, I made the deep "uh" that accompanied my best effort, and Bobo did his job.

"Come on Lily, squeeze, you can do it," he exhorted sternly, and the bar touched my chin. "Look at Lily's definition, Toni," Bobo said over his shoulder. Behind his back, Toni looked at me as if she wished I'd vanish in a puff of smoke. But I was honor-bound to complete the next two reps. When they were done, Bobo said, "You can do another one. You've got it left in you."

"I'm through, thanks," I said firmly. I rose and removed the clips that secured the weights. We began putting the discs back on the rack.

Toni wandered over to the water fountain.

"I need to talk to you this weekend," Bobo said quietly.

"Okay." I hesitated. "Saturday afternoon?"

He nodded. "Your place?"

"All right." I was doubtful about the wisdom of this, but I owed it to him to listen, whatever he wanted to say.

My forehead was beaded with sweat. Instead of searching out my towel, I lifted the hem of my T-shirt and dabbed at my forehead, ensuring Bobo saw the horrendous scars on my ribs.

I saw him gulp. I went on to my next exercise feeling obscurely vindicated. Though Bobo was handsome and wholesome as a loaf of good bread, and I had once or twice been tempted to take a bite, Toni was from his world. I intended to see he kept my age and bitter experience in his mind.

Janet was doing shoulders this morning, and I spotted for her while she worked on the Gravitron. Her knees on the small platform, the counterweight set at forty pounds so she wouldn't be lifting her whole body weight, Janet gripped the bars above her head and pulled up. She was working pretty hard the first few reps, and by number eight, I wandered over to hold her feet and push up gently to lighten the strain on her arms. When she'd finished number ten, Janet dangled from the bars, panting, and after a minute she slid her knees off the platform and stood on the uprights. Stepping off backward, she took a few more seconds to catch her breath and let the muscles of her shoulders recoup.

"Are you going to the funeral?" she asked. She moved the pin to the thirty-pound slot.

"I don't know." I hated the thought of dressing up

and going into the crowded Shakespeare Combined Church. "Have you heard if the time's certain yet?"

"Last night, my mother was over at Lacey and Jerrell's when the funeral home called to say the coroner's office in Little Rock was sending the body back. Lacey said Saturday morning at eleven."

I considered, scowling. I could probably finish work by eleven if I got up extra early and hurried. If I ever got around to getting my clients to sign a contract, I decided one of the clauses would be that I didn't have to go to their funerals.

"I guess I should," I said reluctantly.

"Great!" Janet looked positively happy. "If it's okay with you, I'll park at your house and we can walk to the funeral together."

Making that little arrangement would never have occurred to me. "Okay," I said, struggling not to sound astonished or doubtful. Then I realized I had a bit of news I should share.

"Claude and Carrie got married," I told her.

"You're . . . you're serious!" Janet faced me, astonished. "When?"

"At the courthouse, yesterday."

"Hey, Marshall!" Janet called to our *sensei*, who'd just come out of the office in the hallway between the weight room and the aerobics room where we held karate classes. Marshall turned, holding a glass of some grainy brown stuff he drank for breakfast. Marshall was wearing his normal uniform of T-shirt and muscle pants. He raised his black eyebrows to ask, What?

"Claude and Carrie got married, Lily says!"

This caused a general burst of comment among the

others in the room. Brian Gruber quit doing stomach crunches and sat up on the bench, patting his face with his towel. Jeri yanked her cellular phone from her workout bag and called a friend she knew would be up and drinking her coffee. A couple of other people sauntered over to discuss this news. And I caught a blaze of some emotion on Bobo's face, some feeling I found didn't fit in any category of comfortable response to my trivial piece of gossip.

"How did you know?" Janet asked, and I discovered I was in the middle of a small group of sweaty and curious people.

"I was there," I answered, surprised.

"You were a witness?"

I nodded.

"What did she wear?" Jerri asked, pushing her streaky blond hair away from her forehead.

"Where'd they go for their honeymoon?" asked Marlys Squire, a travel agent with four grandchildren.

"Where are they gonna live?" asked Brian Gruber, who'd been trying to sell his own house for five months.

For a moment, I thought of turning tail and simply walking away, but . . . maybe . . . it wasn't so bad, talking to these people, being part of a group.

But when I was driving away from the gym I felt the reaction; I'd let myself down, somehow, a corner of my brain warned. I'd opened myself, made it easy. Instead of sliding between those people, observing but not participating, I'd held still long enough to be pegged in place, laid myself open to interpretation by giving them a piece of my thoughts.

While I worked that day, I retreated into a deep

silence, comforting and refreshing as an old bathrobe. But it wasn't as comfortable as it had been. It didn't seem, somehow, to fit anymore.

That evening I walked, the cool night covering me with its darkness. I saw Joel McCorkindale, the minister of the Shakespeare Combined Church, running his usual three miles, his charisma turned off for the evening. I observed that Doris Massey, whose husband had died the previous year, had resumed entertaining, since Charles Friedrich's truck was parked in front of her trailer. Clifton Emanuel, Marta Schuster's deputy, rolled by in a dark green Bronco. Two teenagers were breaking into the Bottle and Can Liquor Store, and I used my cell phone to call the police station before I melted into the night. No one saw me; I was invisible.

I was lonely.

SIX

J ack called Friday morning just as I was leaving for my appointment with Lacey at Deedra's apartment.

"I'm on my way back," he said. "Maybe I can come down Sunday afternoon."

I felt a flash of resentment. He'd drive down from Little Rock for the afternoon, we'd hop into bed, and he'd have to go back for work on Monday. I made myself admit that I had to work Monday, too, that even if he stayed in Shakespeare we wouldn't get to see each other that much. Seeing him a little was better than not seeing him at all . . . as of this moment.

"I'll see you then," I said, but my pause had been perceptible and I knew I didn't sound happy enough.

There was a thoughtful silence on the other end of the line. Jack is not stupid, especially where I'm concerned.

"Something's wrong," he said at last. "Can we talk about it when I get there?"

"All right," I said, trying to soften my voice.

"Good-bye." And I hung up, taking care to be gentle with the telephone.

I was a little early. I propped myself against the wall by Deedra's apartment door and waited for Lacey. I was sullen and grim, and I knew that was unreasonable. When Lacey trudged up the stairs, I nodded a greeting, and she seemed just as content to leave it at that.

She'd succeeded in getting Jerrell to remove the boxes we'd packed the previous session, so the apartment looked a lot emptier. After a minimum of discussion, I began sorting through things in the small living room while Lacey boxed the linens.

I pitched all the magazines into a garbage bag and opened the drawer in the coffee table. I saw a roll of mints, a box of pens, some Post-It notes, and the instruction booklet that had come with Deedra's VCR. I patted the bottom of the drawer, then reached back in its depths. That netted me a coupon for a Healthy Choice microwave meal. I frowned, feeling the muscles around my mouth clamp in what would be wrinkles before too many years passed.

"It's gone," I said.

Lacey said, "What?"

I hadn't even heard her in the kitchen behind me. The service hatch was open.

"The *TV Guide.*"

"Maybe you threw it away Wednesday?"

"No," I said positively.

"What possible difference could it make?" Lacey didn't sound dismissive, but she did sound puzzled.

I stood to face her. She was leaning, elbows on the

kitchen counter, her golden-brown sweater already streaked with lint from the dryer. "I don't know," I said, and shrugged. "But Deedra always, always kept the *TV Guide* in this drawer, because she marked the shows she wanted to tape." I'd always found it interesting that someone with Deedra's limited intelligence was blessed with a knack for small appliances. She could set her VCR to tape her favorite shows in a matter of minutes. On nights she didn't have a date, Deedra had television. Even when Deedra was going to be in her apartment, if there was a man present, often she wouldn't watch her shows. She'd set up her VCR to record.

Every workday morning, Deedra slid in a tape to catch her favorite soaps, and sometimes *Oprah*. She used the Post-It notes to label her tapes; there was always a little yellow cloud of them in the living room wastebasket.

Oh, hell, what difference could a missing magazine make? Nothing else was missing—nothing that I'd yet discovered. If Deedra's purse was still missing (and I hadn't heard that it had been found) then the thief hadn't been after her keys for entry into her apartment, but had wanted something else in her purse.

I couldn't imagine what that object could be. And there wasn't anything of value missing from the apartment, only the stupid *TV Guide*. Oh, there might be some Kleenex missing. I hadn't counted those. Marta would probably ask me to.

While I'd been grumbling to myself, I'd been running my hands under the bright floral couch cushions, crouching to look underneath the little skirt that concealed the legs.

"It's just not here," I concluded. Lacey had come into the living room. She was looking at me with a puzzled expression.

"Did you want it for something special?" she asked cautiously, obviously humoring me.

I felt like a fool. "It's the only thing that's missing," I explained. "Marta Schuster asked me to tell her if I found anything gone missing, and the *TV Guide* is the only thing."

"I just hardly see . . ." Lacey said doubtfully.

"Me too. But I guess I better call her."

Marta Schuster was out of the office, so I talked to Deputy Emanuel. He promised to draw the absence of the magazine to Sheriff Schuster's attention. But the way he said it told me he thought I was crazy for reporting the missing *TV Guide*. And I couldn't blame him for his conclusion.

As I went back to my work, it occurred to me that only a maid would have noticed the absence of the *TV Guide*. And I had to admit to myself that I'd only noticed because once Deedra had left it on the couch and I'd put it on the kitchen counter: in the hatchway, though, so it was easily visible. But Deedra had had a fit, one of the very few she'd had while I'd cleaned for her. She'd told me in no uncertain terms that the *TV Guide* always, always went in the coffee-table drawer.

So a mad rapist molests Deedra, strangles her, parks her nude in her car out in the woods and . . . steals her *TV Guide*? *TV Guides* were readily available in at least five places in Shakespeare. Why would anyone need Deedra's? I snorted, and put the thought aside to work over some other time. But Deedra herself wouldn't leave my

76

thoughts. That was only right, I admitted to myself reluctantly. I'd cleaned her apartment for four years; I knew many tiny details about her life that no one else knew. That's the thing with cleaning people's homes; you absorb a lot of information with that cleaning. There's nothing more revealing about people than the mess they leave for someone else. The only people who get to see a home unprepared and unguarded are a maid, a burglar, and a policeman.

I wondered which of the men Deedra had bedded had decided she had to die. Or had it been an impulse? Had she refused to perform some particular act, had she threatened to inform someone's wife that he was straying, had she clung too hard? Possible, all three scenarios, but not probable. As far as I knew there was nothing Deedra would refuse to do sexually, she'd steered clear of married men for the most part, and if she'd valued one bedmate over another I'd never known about it.

The sheriff's brother could've been different. He was attractive, and he'd certainly carried on like he was crazy about Deedra.

Deedra would sure have been an embarrassing sister-in-law for Marta Schuster. I was lying on the floor checking to make sure nothing else was underneath Deedra's couch when that unwelcome thought crossed my mind. I stayed down for a moment, turning the idea back and forth, chewing at it.

I nearly discarded it out of hand. Marta was tough enough to handle embarrassment. And from my reading of the situation, I felt Marlon had just begun his relationship with Deedra; there was no other way to explain his extravagant display of grief. He was young enough to have illusions, and maybe he'd dodged the talk about Deedra with enough agility to have hope she'd cleave only to him, to put a biblical spin on it.

Perhaps she would have. After all, Deedra hadn't been smart, but even Deedra must have seen that she couldn't go on as she had been. Right?

Maybe she'd never let herself think of the future. Maybe, once started on her course, she'd been content to just drift along? I felt a rush of contempt.

Then I wondered what I myself had been doing for the past six years.

As I rose to my knees and then to my feet, I argued to myself that I'd been learning to survive—to not go crazy—every single day since I'd been raped and knifed.

Standing in Deedra Dean's living room, listening to her mother working down the hall, I realized that I was no longer in danger of craziness, though I supposed I'd have fits of anxiety the rest of my days. I had made a life, I had earned my living, and I had bought a house of my own. I had insurance. I drove a car and paid taxes. I had mastered survival. For a long moment I stood staring through the hatchway into Deedra's fluorescently bright kitchen, thinking what a strange time and place it was to realize such a large thing.

And since I was in her apartment, I had to think of Deedra again. She'd been slaughtered before she'd had time to come through whatever was making her behave the way she did. Her body had been degraded—displayed naked, and violated. Though I had not let myself think of it before now, I had a mental picture of the Coca-Cola bottle protruding from Deedra's vagina. I wondered if

78

she'd been alive when that had happened. I wondered if she'd had time to know.

I felt dizzy suddenly, almost sick, so I plopped down on the couch and stared at my hands. I'd gotten too wrapped up in my inner depiction of Deedra's last minutes. I was remembering the hours in the shack in the fields, the hours I'd spent chained to an old iron bedstead, waiting to die, almost longing for it. I thought of the sickness of the phone calls Deedra had been getting right before she was killed. There are men who should die, I thought.

"Lily? Are you all right?" Lacey leaned over me, her face concerned.

I yanked myself back to the moment. "Yes," I said stiffly. "Thank you. I'm sorry."

"You're sick?"

"I have an inner ear problem. I just got dizzy for a second," I lied. It made me uncomfortable, lying, but it was easier on Lacey than the truth.

She went back to her task, casting an uneasy look back at me, and I began going through the tapes Deedra had had around the television, making sure there weren't any pornographic ones mixed in with the ones marked ALL MY CHILDREN or SALLY JESSY ON THURSDAY. These tapes were all presumably still usable. I figured I'd make sure there wasn't anything risqué on them, and asked Lacey if I could use the tapes. As I expected, she agreed, and I packed them in a box without finishing my evaluation. If I found anything objectionable in the tapes, I could pitch them at home more easily. Just another little cleanup job to complete.

We can't leave this world without leaving a lot of detritus behind. We never go out as cleanly as we come in; and even when we come in, there's the afterbirth.

I looked forward to karate that night more than I had in weeks. So much reflection, so much unwelcome remembrance needed to be worked out of my system. I liked to *do,* not reflect: I wanted to kick some butt so badly I ached. That's not the right way to approach the discipline, and that's not the correct mind frame for martial arts. My body twanged with tension as I took my place in line.

Attendance at the Friday-night classes tended to be a bit lighter than at the Monday and Wednesday classes. Tonight there were only ten people stretching at the barres along the wall. Bobo bowed at the doorway and strolled into the room in a white tank top and the pants-half of his *gi.* His girlfriend, Toni, had tagged along. Bobo kicked off his sandals and got into line two people down from me, pulling Toni in beside him. She was wearing black shorts and a purple T-shirt, and she'd pinned her dark hair back with an elastic band and a million hairpins. She was trying to look comfortable.

As always, Becca was first in line. She'd stretched on her own before class, smiling at Carlton when he wandered over to talk to her, but not saying much herself. Raphael, usually on my left, was at a dance; he and his wife were chaperoning his daughter's Spring Fling at the high school. He'd told me he thought some of the restraining moves Marshall had taught us might come in handy if the boys went out in the parking lot to drink.

"You and Lacey 'bout done cleaning out Deedra's place?" Becca asked as we waited to be called to attention.

"We haven't finished yet. But a lot of boxes are gone. Just a little left to pack, and the big stuff can be moved out."

She nodded, and was about to say something else when Marshall put on his hardest face and barked, *"Kiotske!"*

We came to attention and exchanged bows with him. "Line up for sit-ups!"

Becca and I usually paired up, since we were much the same weight and height. I moved to stand facing her and checked to make sure everyone in my new line had a partner. Then Becca and I sat down facing each other, legs extended in front of us and slightly bent at the knees. Becca slid her feet between mine and turned them outward to hook under my calves. I turned my feet in to latch on to hers.

Marshall had motioned Bobo's girlfriend, Toni, to pair with Janet, who was much closer to Toni's size than Bobo. Bobo, in turn, had to make do with the only man approaching him in height and weight, Carlton. The two men of the world, I thought, and watched as Bobo and Carlton silently contended over who got to be "outie" and who got to be "innie." Becca and I grinned at each other as Carlton slid his legs between Bobo's, who'd held out the longest.

"Put your hands under your butts, like this!" Marshall held up his hands so Toni could see. The index finger of his right hand touched the index finger of the left, and the opposing thumbs touched each other, but the matching pairs were spread as far apart as possible. "Your tailbone should be in the open space. Let yourselves lie back, but don't touch the floor!" Marshall ordered, being specific since we had a visitor. He strolled down the line with his thumbs hooked in his obi. He examined himself in one of the mirrors that lined the wall, and smoothed his black hair with one ivory hand. Marshall's one-quarter-Asian blood was his favorite fraction, and he did everything he could to emphasize his otherness. He thought it made him more effective and attractive as a *sensei* and a gym owner if he looked exotic, or as exotic as southern Arkansas would tolerate. He was right.

Meanwhile, Becca and I tucked our hands under our respective butts and leaned back very slowly, mirroring each other, until our shoulders were about two inches from the floor. I was looking at the ceiling, concentrating on the crack I always used to focus my attention. With the pull from our linked legs providing an anchor, we would be able to maintain this excruciating position for an indeterminate time. I rolled my eyes sideways to check out what our *sensei* was doing. He was straightening his *gi.* Bobo, right beside me, met my eyes and shook his head slightly in mock despair. Carlton, beside Becca, had already broken into a sweat.

I made a tiny, derisive sound, just loud enough to carry to our *sensei*. Marshall was preening while we were hurting, and the weakest of us would be worn out by the time we started the exercise.

"On my count!" Marshall barked, and we all tensed. Carlton was trembling, and Toni, hooked to Janet, seemed totally unable to pull up off the floor, where her entire body was firmly settled. At least she was providing good ballast for her partner.

"One, two, three, four, five, six, seven, eight, nine, ten! One, two, three, four, five, six, seven, eight, nine, twenty! One, two . . ." With each count we tightened our abdominals, then relaxed them, our upper bodies rising perhaps six inches off the floor to relax down to two on the off count. Our row bobbed frantically to keep up, abdominals rigid with the effort of keeping our backs off the floor. I glanced to the right, checking my half of the row, since Marshall might ask me to correct their faults. Carlton and Toni were side by side on Becca's row, which pleased me. Bobo looked to his left just then, and our eyes met. He grinned at me. He thought this was great fun. He had to have found another dojo in Montrose, to be in such good shape. I shook my head in wry amazement, and turned my concentration back to my own work. I closed my eyes and kept up with the count, knowing Becca would never give up and go slack.

"Get your elbows off the floor!" Marshal admonished, and the two new boys at the end of the row gasped and obeyed. I scowled at the ceiling as I heard the thud of a head hitting the floor only seconds later. That was on my side, and it was one of the new boys. After a few half-hearted attempts to make his abdominals obey, he openly gave up, and he and Toni did fish imitations together, mouths open and gasping. Toni had lasted maybe the first set of ten. Obviously, Bobo hadn't met her in a gym.

Finally, only Bobo, Becca, and I were still going.

"One hundred!" Marshall said, and stopped. We three froze with our backs off the floor. I could hear Becca breathing loudly, and tried not to smile.

"Hold it!" commanded Marshall, and with an effort of will, I stayed up.

"Hold it!" he exhorted us. I began to tremble.

"Relax," he said, and it was all I could do not to let myself collapse with the same embarrassing thud. I managed to detach my legs from Becca's and let my shoulders and back ease to the floor without any urgency. I hoped.

Ragged breathing filled the room. I turned to look at Bobo. He was beaming at me from a couple of feet away.

"How ya doing, Lily?" he gasped.

"I could have done thirty more," I said with no conviction. He giggled weakly.

Marshall didn't tell us to put on sparring pads tonight. At least partly because of Toni's presence (even the students we called "the new boys" had been coming a month) he decided to instruct us to practice breaking away. There were about four simple moves that each new class member had to learn. While the other people practiced more sophisticated maneuvers, I was set to teach these moves to Toni. She protested nervously several times that she was just visiting with Bobo—probably she would never come to class again. I just kept on instructing her. No one (least of all the timid Toni) would quite dare to just tell Marshall *no*. At least, no one I'd ever met.

My estimation of the girl rose as I worked with her. She gave it her best shot, though she was obviously uncomfortable with being in the class at all. I could like that determination—admire it, even.

"God, you're strong," she said, trying not to sound angry, as I gripped her wrists and told her to practice the breaking-free method I'd just taught her.

"I've been working at this for years."

"You're some kind of hero to Bobo," she said, her eyes fixed on me to see how I'd react.

I had no idea how to respond to that. I wanted to ignore what Toni had said, but she refused to move when

I took her wrist, playing my role of attacker. She just waited, her face turned up to mine.

"I'm not a hero in any sense," I said curtly. "Now, break free from my hold!"

I got out of there fast when class was over. Janet had left even faster after letting me know she had a date, so she wasn't there to chat with me on my way out, and the weight room was almost empty. I thought I heard Bobo call my name, but I kept marching forward. I'd see him tomorrow afternoon, anyway.

SEVEN

I was exhausted, but I couldn't sleep. There was no point in tearing up my bed tossing and turning any longer. In the darkness I slid into my jeans, black sports bra, an old black Nike T-shirt, and my sneakers. My keys and cell phone were always in the same place on my dresser; I pocketed them and slipped out the front door to begin walking.

There had been too many nights of this pointless activity, I reflected. Too many nights of striding through a silent town—for the past few years this particular silent town of Shakespeare. Before that, other towns in other states: Tennessee, Mississippi. My feet moved silently on the pavement as I covered ground.

I seldom felt the compulsion to walk when Jack stayed with me. If I was restless, I satisfied that restlessness in a more intimate way. Tonight I felt worn ragged, and old.

One of the town's night patrolmen, Gardner Mc-Clanahan, saluted me as he cruised slowly by. He knew better than to stop and talk. Though Claude would never have told me, I'd heard the town police called me the Night Walker, a pun on the title of an old TV show. Every patrol officer knew I'd anonymously called in at least five break-ins and three domestic situations, but we'd silently agreed to pretend they didn't know their tipster was me. After the previous year, they all knew about my past. I thought it very strange that they apparently respected me for it.

I didn't raise my hand to acknowledge Gardner, as I would some nights. I kept on moving.

Forty minutes later, I'd circled, doubled, gone to all four points of the compass, and still was only about six blocks from home. On Main, I was passing Joe C's house, thinking once again about its size and age, when I stopped in my tracks. Had that been a flicker of movement among the bushes in the yard of the Prader house? My hand dropped to the cell phone in my pocket, but there was no point calling the police if I'd been mistaken. I slunk into the yard myself, moving through the overgrown shrubbery as silently as I could.

Yes. Ahead of me, someone was moving. Someone all in black. Someone quiet and quick like me. The closest streetlight was half a block away and the yard was deep and shadowy.

It took me only seconds to realize that whoever this trespasser was, he was moving away from the house, not toward it. I wondered if he'd been trying the doors, hoping to enter and steal. I began making my way as quietly as I could through the jungle of Joe C's yard.

Then I smelled smoke. I froze in position, my head

rotating to track from which direction the thick dark scent was pouring.

It was coming from the house. My skin began to crawl with apprehension. Not even attempting quiet movement, I pressed close enough to peer through the open curtains of Joe C's living room, the room I'd vacuumed just three days before. Now that I was out of the bushes, the streetlight gave me a little visibility. There were no lights on in the house, but I should have been able to see the outlines of the furniture. Instead, there was a dense movement inside the room. After a second, I realized the room was full of smoke; it was coiling against the windows, waiting to be let out. As I stared into the dark moving cloud, I saw the first dart of the flames.

I broke into a run, crashing through the overgrown crepe myrtles and camellias, around the house and up the shaky steps to Joe C's back door. I'd decided the back door was farthest from the fire. There was no time to waste trying to track the trespasser. As I pounded on the door to wake the old man, I pulled the phone out of my pocket and dialed 911.

I told the dispatcher what the situation was, and she answered, "We'll be there in a minute, Lily," which I'd probably find amusing another time. The smell of smoke was increasing by the second. I pocketed the phone and forced myself to touch the doorknob. It wasn't hot. Though I expected the door would be locked, it opened easily.

A cloud of darkness billowed out. With it came the terrible smell of things being consumed by fire. I was gasping with terror, knowing I had to try to reach Joe C.

I hesitated, shamefully, afraid of being trapped if I went in. I knew the door must be shut behind me to prevent cross breezes from fanning the flames. For a long second, I was awfully tempted to shut myself right back out on the porch. But that was just something I couldn't do. I took a deep breath of clean air. Then I entered the burning house and closed the opening to safety.

I started to switch on the lights, realized I shouldn't. In the choking gloom, I made my way across the kitchen to the familiar double sink, felt the dishcloth draped across the divider. I rinsed it out under cold water and held it across my mouth and nose as I tried to fumble my way out of the kitchen and across the hall to Joe C's bedroom.

I sucked in breath to call the old man, and that breath exploded out in a bout of coughing. I saw flames to my right, in the living room. Smoke, a deadly silent killer, filled the wide hall. I put one hand to the wall to orient myself, touching a picture of Joe C's mother I recalled was hanging about a yard to the left of the door to Joe C's bedroom. I could hear sirens now, but no coughing from anyone but me.

"Joe C!" I screamed, the intake of smoke causing me another coughing spasm. I might have heard something in reply. At least I imagined that I heard a faint answer after I gave a second call. The fire was in the living room, moving closer to the hall, licking at something it really liked. I could feel a sudden escalation in its energy, as if it had eaten a piece of candy. Maybe it had grabbed ahold of Joe C's antique rolltop desk, its wood dry and ready for the flame after a hundred and fifty years of use.

The door to Joe C's bedroom was closed. I didn't

know if that was usual or not. I turned the knob, and it opened. I was having good luck with doors tonight, if nothing else.

"Joe C," I called hoarsely. "Where are you?" I stepped cautiously into the bedroom and shut the door behind me.

"Here," came the feeble reply. "I'm trying to open this damn winda."

Since Joe C's bedroom and the kitchen were at the back of the house, away from the streetlight, between the smoke and the natural darkness I couldn't tell exactly where the old man was.

"Say something!" I began groping my way into the room, colliding with the bedpost as I shuffled forward. That gave me my bearings.

Joe C said a few things, none of them repeatable.

Finally I reached him, hearing him begin to cough so violently that I knew he didn't have long to go if we stayed inside. I followed his hands up to the two locks on the window, and I took over the job of twisting them. The right one was easy, the left one very stiff. I wrestled with it, decided to break the glass in about one second if the lock didn't give.

"Damn, woman, get us out of here!" Joe C said urgently. "The fire is at the door!" Then he was overwhelmed by another coughing spasm.

I glanced over my shoulder to see that the door appeared to be cracking, and the cracks had red edges. If I touched that doorknob now, my hands would burn.

As my whole body would if the damn window . . . there! The lock gave, I reached down to grip the handles, and I heaved up with all my strength. The window, which

I had expected to resist, flew up, and I almost lost my footing. I stuck my hand outward to feel, and encountered a screen. Crap.

I took a step back, lifted my leg, and let it fly. The screen popped out of the window like a cork from a bottle, and I said, between bouts of a hacking cough, "I'm going out first, and then I'm getting you over the sill, Joe C."

He clung to me, still no more than part of the choking darkness, and I had to disengage his hands to swing my leg over the sill. Of course the bushes were thick underneath the window, and since the house was raised, the drop-off was at least a foot higher than I'd anticipated. I didn't land square on my feet, but careened sideways, grabbing at branches so I wouldn't end up on the ground. When my footing was stabilized, I turned and felt through the window until I had run my hands under both Joe C's armpits.

"Hold on to my shoulders!" I urged him, and his bony claws dug into my skin. I put my left foot somewhat back to keep me steady, and I heaved. Because of the high window, the angle was bad; I was too short to get a good purchase. I gradually worked Joe C about halfway out the window. He began hollering. I took two steps back and heaved again, my shoulders in agony from the strain. More of the old man appeared on my side of the window. I repeated the whole process. But now Joe C began yelling in earnest. I craned over his back to see that his left foot remained hooked to the sill in some mysterious way.

I had a moment of sheer panic. I could not think for the life of me—for *his* life—how I was going to extricate him. Luckily, I didn't have to solve the problem. There was commotion all around me now. I was never happier to see anyone in my life than the firefighter who pushed past me to unhook Joe C's left foot and bring it out to join the rest of him. I staggered back under Joe C's full weight, and instantly men were helping me to stand, whisking the old man over to ambulance.

They tried to load me in, too, but I resisted. I'm no martyr, but I can only afford minimal insurance, and I could manage to stand and walk.

I sat on the tailgate of the fire chief's pickup while a couple of firefighters gave me oxygen, which felt sweet to my lungs. They checked me over; not a single burn. I reeked of smoke and didn't think I would ever breathe easily again, but those were minor considerations right now. At least six firefighters told me how lucky I was. They also mentioned that I should have waited for their help in extricating Joe C. I just nodded; I think we all knew that if I'd waited, Joe C wouldn't have had much of a chance.

When they were sure I was going to be all right, the two men who'd been tending to me went to help with the more exciting activity across the street. I didn't know if they'd be able to put out the fire before the first floor collapsed, but it was clear Joe C was not going to get his often-stated wish of dying in his own home.

Gradually, though the hubbub around me continued, I was able to think about something other than how afraid I'd been. I was able to think about what I'd seen.

"You feeling better?" demanded a nasal voice.

I nodded without looking up.

"Then you want to tell me how you came to be here?"

My questioner was Norman Farraclough, Claude's second in command. He was called "Jump" Farraclough, the result of a story I'd never completely understood. I'd encountered Jump several times. He always seemed to be holding any judgment about me in reserve until he'd observed me a little longer. Actually, that was pretty much the same way I felt about him.

Jump was a late-night weightlifter, when his shift permitted. He often arrived at Body Time just when I was leaving karate class. The assistant police chief had a sharp hooked nose, a tiny mustache, and a pumped body that looked awkward in his blue uniform.

The fire chief, Frank Parrish, holding his helmet by one strap, came to stand by Jump, and they both looked down at me with expectant faces.

I explained very slowly how I'd come to be passing Joe C's house. Slowly, because not only was breathing still an act I wasn't taking for granted, but also I wanted to be sure I didn't make any error, any ambiguous statement, in what I was telling them. I told Jump and Frank about seeing someone in the yard, smelling the smoke, and finding the back door unlocked.

Jump's face remained expressionless, but Frank was openly troubled by my story.

"Was it a man or a woman?" he asked when I'd come to the end.

"Couldn't tell."

"Which direction did he go in?"

"Towards the back of the yard, but there's no fence back there. He could've gone anywhere after that."

"And that back door was unlocked?"

I sighed, tried to keep it inaudible. "Yes." It was the third time Frank had asked me.

"You work for Joe C, right?" Jump squatted down to

my level to look me directly in the eyes. If this was supposed to be intimidating, it didn't work.

"Yes."

"You and him get along?"

"He's a dirty old bastard," I said.

And that shocked them, me saying out loud what everyone on God's green earth already knew.

"But you went in to the house to get him?"

"Obviously I did." Though I was beginning to regret it.

"That lot is worth a right smart piece of change," Frank observed to the night air.

I had no response to that. I wanted to shower, to get the stink of smoke off me. I never wanted to smell it again.

"I'm going home." I stood and began walking.

"Whoa, just a minute!" Jump got into step beside me. "Listen, lady, you ain't got no privileges now, with your buddy gone."

"You're talking about your *boss*? The boss whose wedding I just attended? As his bride's *best friend*?" This behavior wasn't typical of me, but I was going to pull every string I could to get away from this fire, away from the old house and the smoke.

"Doesn't cut any ice with me," Jump stated, but I didn't believe him.

"Your testosterone's showing," I told him. He glanced down before he could stop himself. "I saw a fire, I reported it like a good citizen, and I helped an old man escape death. You can make something suspicious out of that if you want, but I don't think it's gonna fly." And I lengthened my stride, leaving him standing and staring after me with baffled irritation on his shadowed face.

EIGHT

I slept late the next day. I must have punched down my alarm button without even knowing it, because when I finally checked the clock, I saw that I was supposed to be at my first Saturday morning cleaning job. I left my bed unmade, my breakfast uneaten, and arrived at Carrie's office barefaced and groggy. There was no one there to see me in any condition at all, so I accelerated my pace and got her office finished, then scooted over to the travel agent's.

I'd gotten my adrenaline pumping so effectively that I actually finished early. When I got home I collapsed at my kitchen table, trying to figure out what the rest of the day held. My Saturdays were usually spent grocery shopping and cleaning my own place. I tried to recall what else I had going.

Well, there was Deedra's funeral. Janet was coming by within the hour to accompany me to that. Then Bobo was coming over for some unstated purpose. And I still had to shop and clean since Jack was driving in tomorrow.

All I wanted to do was sleep, or rent a movie and sit in a silent lump on my double recliner to watch it. But I hoisted myself to my feet and went to the bathroom for a hot shower.

When Janet thumped on my front door forty-five minutes later, I was in my black suit, made up, with hose and pumps making me feel like a stranger to myself. I had just completed my makeup, and as I opened the door to her, I was pushing the back onto my left earring.

"Lily, you look good in black," Janet said.

"Thanks. You're looking good yourself." It was true; Janet was wearing a chestnut sheath with a brown-gold-green jacket, and it brought out the best in her coloring and figure.

It was time to go, so I grabbed my purse and locked the door on the way out.

"Oh, by the way," Janet said, "I told Becca we'd stop by the apartments and pick her up."

I shrugged. Why anyone needed to be accompanied to a funeral was outside of my understanding, but I had no objection.

Becca came out of the big front doors of the Shakespeare Garden Apartments just as we walked up. She was wearing a dark blue dress with big white polka dots, and she'd put up her hair somehow under a navy blue straw hat. With her usual dramatic makeup, Becca looked as if she had a bit part in a film about charming Southern eccentrics.

"Hidey!" she said, all perky and upbeat. I stared at her. "Sorry," Becca told us after a second. "I've got to sober down. I just got a real good piece of news, and I haven't got it out of my system."

"Can we ask?" asked Janet. Her round brown eyes were almost protruding with curiosity.

"Well," Becca said, looking as though she'd blush with pleasure if Revlon hadn't already done it for her, "my brother is coming to see me."

Janet and I exchanged significant glances. Becca had only mentioned her brother Anthony a time or two, and Janet had wondered aloud one time why the apartments had been left to Becca. Why not a fair split between sister and brother? I hadn't responded, because it was none of my business how Pardon Albee had left his estate, but I had had to admit to myself that singling out Becca had seemed a little unusual. Now we'd get to meet the brother, maybe discover why Becca had been so favored.

In a polite voice, Janet said, "That's real nice." We were too close to the church to keep the discussion open.

Distracted by Becca's surprising mood and news, I hadn't noticed that our small street was very nearly in a state of gridlock. Cars were parked on both sides of Track Street and around the corner, as far as I could see. Track Street is the base of three streets laid out like a U tipped on its left side. Estes Arboretum fills up the empty part of the U, and the Shakespeare Combined Church is on the upper bar. It's a fundamentalist Christian church with a pastor, Joel McCorkindale, who can raise money like nobody's business. Joel is handsome and shiny, like a country-and-western star, with his razor-cut hair and perfect white teeth. He's added a mustache trimmed so precisely that it looks as though he could chop his meat with it.

The SCC, as the Shakespeareans call it, has added two wings in the past three years. There's a day care, a pre-school, and a basketball gym for the teenagers. I was assuming they found time to have church on Sundays, sandwiched somewhere between Singles Hour, Teen Handbells, and classes like How to Please your Husband in a Christian Marriage. I've worked there from time to time, and the Reverend McCorkindale and I have had some interesting conversations.

The steeple bell was tolling heavily as we three strode up the gentle slope that leveled off in front of the church. The white hearse of Shields Funeral Home was lined up with its white limousine parallel to the curb directly in front of the church, and through the smoked windows of the limousine I could make out the family waiting to enter. Though I didn't want to stare at them, I couldn't seem to help it. Lacey looked stricken and hopeless. Jerrell looked resigned.

Janet, Becca, and I entered the main doors and were escorted by an usher to our seats. I made sure Becca went first so he grasped her arm instead of mine. The church was packed with pale people in dark clothes. The family pews, with the front one left empty for Lacey and Jerrell, were filled with all the cousins and aunts and uncles of the dead woman, and I picked out Bobo's bright hair beside the dark head of Calla Prader. I had forgotten that Deedra was Bobo's cousin.

The usher gestured us into the end of a pew about midway down the church. It was a good thing we'd come when we had, since it was the last place open that could accommodate three people. Janet glanced around the sanctuary with curiosity. Becca studied the program the usher had handed us. I wished I were somewhere else, anywhere. Jack would be here tomorrow and there was a lot I needed to do; I was worried about his visit, about the problems we faced. The scent of the banks of flowers filled the air of the church, already challenged by all these people, and my head began to ache.

Joel McCorkindale, in a black robe with even blacker velvet bands striping the sleeves, appeared at the front of the church after the organ had droned through several gloomy pieces. We all rose, and with due professional solemnity the team from the funeral home (one male Shields and one female Shields) wheeled the coffin down the aisle. After the casket came the pallbearers, two by two, each wearing a carnation in his lapel and walking slowly with eyes downcast. All the pallbearers were male, and as I scanned their faces I wondered how many of them had performed intimate acts with the body in the coffin preceding them. It was a grotesque thought. I wasn't proud of myself for entertaining it. Most of them were older men, men the age of Jerrell and Lacey, who were coming in at the pallbearers' heels.

Lacey was clinging to Jerrell, and he had to give her a lot of help just to make it to the front pew. As the couple went past the rest of the family, it occurred to me to wonder why Becca was sitting beside me instead of on the other side of the church. She was a cousin of Deedra's, too, though she'd had little chance to get to know her.

It had been a crowded week for the Prader/Dean/Winthrop/Albee clan. I wondered how many of them were thinking of the burning of Joe C's house the night before instead of the murder of the woman in the casket.

A few more people slipped in at the back before the

ushers closed the doors. The church was packed to capacity. Not only was Deedra too young to die, she had been murdered. So perhaps the curiosity factor had a part to play in this crowd.

Maybe because I was stifling—the press of people and the heavy scent of flowers almost overwhelmed me—I found myself wondering if my own funeral would have been as well attended if I'd died when I'd been abducted years before. It was all too easy to imagine my parents following the coffin in, and I could even be pretty sure who my pallbearers would have been. . . .

I yanked myself back to the here-and-now. There was something sickly self-indulgent about reviewing my own funeral.

The ceremony continued about like I'd expected. We listened to two singers plow through two old standards, "Amazing Grace" and "What a Friend We Have in Jesus." Since I can sing myself, the performances were interesting, but no more than that. No one here in Shakespeare knew that I used to sing at weddings and funerals in my little hometown, and that was just fine with me. I was better than the woman who sang "Amazing Grace," but my range wasn't as good as the girl who performed second.

I sighed and recrossed my legs. Janet kept her gaze fixed properly on the singers, and Becca examined her cuticles and removed a fragment of thread from the setting of her diamond dinner ring.

I might have known Joel McCorkindale would not let the occasion pass with a simple eulogy, if he'd decided there was a point to be made. To no one's surprise, he based his sermon on the passage in Thessalonians where

Paul warns us that the day of Lord will come like a thief in the night.

The preacher made more of a meal of it than I'd expected. His point was that someone had usurped God's rights in taking Deedra's life. I found myself growing stern and affronted. He was taking away the focus of the funeral from Deedra, who was actually the dead person, and focusing on the man who'd killed her.

To my alarm, the people in the congregation who were used to his style of preaching began to agree audibly with his points. Every now and then a man or a woman would raise hands above head and say, "Amen! Praise the Lord!"

I turned my head slightly to check out Janet's reaction. Her eyes were about to pop out of her head, and she gave them a significant roll when she saw me match her own astonishment. I had never been in a church where it was the norm for the congregation to speak out loud, and by Janet's facial expression, neither had she. Becca, on the other hand, was smiling slightly, as if the whole thing was performance art staged for her benefit.

I could tell the men and women who ordinarily attended this church were very comfortable with this, this . . . audience participation. But I was horribly embarrassed, and when I saw Lacey leaning forward in her seat, hands clasped above her head, tears rolling down her face, I almost got up and left. I never talked to God myself, having gotten out of the inclination for faith after that summer in Memphis; but if I did have such a conversation, I knew it would be in private and no one around me would know. In fact, I promised myself that.

Janet and I were so glad when the service was over

that it was all we could do not to bolt from the church. Becca seemed intrigued with the whole experience.

"Have you ever seen anything like that before?" she asked, but not in a voice low enough to suit me. We were still close to the other mourners, who were scattering to climb into their cars for the drive to the cemetery.

Janet shook her head silently.

"Who knows what'll happen at the gravesite," Becca said in happy anticipation.

"You'll have to catch a ride with Carlton," I said, nodding toward my neighbor who was just coming out of the church. "I'm going home." I started down the sidewalk. Janet trotted after me.

"Hold up, Lily!" she said. "I don't think I'll go to the cemetery either. That service kind of shook me up. I guess Methodists are too repressed for something that emotionally . . . open."

" 'Open,' " I snarled, and kept on walking. "I didn't like that."

"You mean the church? The people?"

I nodded.

"Well, I wasn't raised that way either, but it seemed to make them feel better," Janet commented cautiously. "I don't know, it might have been kind of comforting."

I shuddered.

"Listen, what are you going to do now?"

"Call the hospital."

"About what?"

"Joe C."

"Oh, yeah, he had a fire last night, didn't he?"

I nodded. "See you later," I told Janet. I forced myself to add, "Thanks for going with me."

Janet looked happier. "You're welcome. Thanks for letting me use your driveway." She got into her red Toyota and started it up, waving at me as she backed out.

The street was filled with cars pulling away from the curb, lining up to follow the hearse to the cemetery. As I stood in my front doorway, the street emptied of all its life like one of those time-lapse films. Only one Jeep remained parked farther up the street. I was alone with the trees in the arboretum across the street.

No, not quite alone. As I finally took a step back into my house I saw a man get out of the Jeep and begin to saunter down the street toward me.

It was Bobo, I realized with some astonishment, and remembered our appointment. As he walked, he was loosening his tie and pulling it off, stuffing it into the pocket of his dark suit. He loosened his collar button with two tan fingers, and raked back his blond hair.

Suddenly the postfuneral exaltation of being alive hit me. I felt the crackle of lightning about to strike. The man coming down the sidewalk toward me felt it too. He quickened his pace until he was actually hurrying, keeping all his attention focused on me. When he got to my door, without saying a word he wrapped me in his long arms and held me to him and kissed the hell out of me.

My brain said, *pull away!* But my body wasn't listening. My fingers were twining in Bobo's hair, my pelvis was pressed firmly against his, and I was kissing him back as hard as I could.

We were visible to any passersby.

That must have occurred to Bobo, too, because he pushed me a little and into my house we lurched and he spared a hand to press the door closed.

105

Bobo bit me on the neck and I growled and began grinding into him. The top of my suit was unbuttoned and his hand was inside, caressing me through my bra. Bobo ground right back, and my hands went under his suit coat to hold on to his butt, and our rhythm went on, and somehow he hit exactly the right spot and I saw stars. He groaned, and I felt the front of his pants grow wet.

Then there was only the sound of our panting.

"Floor," Bobo suggested, and our knees gave way.

My living room isn't large and there isn't much floor space. I was sitting right next to the sprawled-out young man, and my blood was still humming through my veins.

But after only a few seconds, I was overwhelmed with the wrongness and stupidity of what I'd just done. And with someone I thought of as a friend. The day before Jack was returning.

All these years of trying so hard not to make a mistake had just gone down the drain.

"Lily," said a voice gently. Bobo was propped up on his elbow next to me. His flushed face had returned to its normal coloring, his breathing was even. His big hand traveled an infinite distance to hold mine. "Lily, don't feel sad."

I was unable to speak. I wondered if Bobo was twenty-one yet. I told myself in the nastiest terms what a depraved moron I had been. I wanted to literally beat my head against the wall.

"It was the moment," he said.

I took a deep breath. "Yes," I answered.

"Don't be so upset," he repeated. "I don't wanna be crude, Lily, but it was just a dry hump."

I'd never heard the phrase before.

"You almost smiled, I saw your mouth twitch," he told me, pleased.

I brushed his hair back from his forehead.

"Can we pretend it never happened?" My voice wasn't as shaky as I'd feared it would be.

"No, I don't think so. What it was, was fantastic. I've always had a thing about you." He drew my hand to him, kissed it. "But I never saw this coming. It was just funeral fever. You know—she's dead, but we're alive. Sex is a great way to prove to yourself you're alive."

"You're being wise."

"It's about time you got a break, let someone else do the wise thing."

"I do plenty of things that aren't so smart," I said, unable to keep the bitterness from my voice.

"Lily, this won't happen again, not ever. You're not gonna let it. So let's be real honest with each other."

I wasn't sure what that would entail. I waited for him to go on.

"There's no telling how many fantasies I've had about you since you worked for my mother. When you know some beautiful, mysterious woman is cleaning your room, it's just a sure thing you're going to imagine . . . what if? My favorite one—"

"Please, no," I said.

"Oh, all right." He had the grace to look a little embarrassed. "But the point of this is I *know* . . . I know it was just a fantasy, that you're real, that we're not gonna have a relationship. I know that you just like me as a . . . buddy."

A little more than that, I thought ruefully. But I knew better than to say it out loud. "You don't really know me," I said, as gently as I was able.

"There's a lot I know about you that you won't admit about yourself," he retorted.

I didn't understand.

"You pull old men out of burning buildings. You saved Jack Leeds' life and almost died in the act. You're willing, and brave enough, to risk your life to save others."

What a misconception! "No, no, no," I protested angrily. He made a kind of dampening gesture, patting down the air with his free hand. I sat up and reached over to the pile of folded laundry on the chair, laundry I hadn't had a chance to put away today. I passed him a hand towel, and he began dabbing at the front of his pants, trying hard not to be embarrassed.

"You did those things. You are brave." He sounded flat, and final.

I didn't want to hear a booster speech from Bobo Winthrop. I was going to feel bad about what had just happened for a long, long time.

"And you're smart, and hard working, and really, really, pretty."

All of a sudden, tears stung the back of my eyelids. The final humiliation, I thought.

"You have to leave," I said abruptly. I leaned over to kiss Bobo on his cheek. For the last—and only—time, I pulled him close and hugged him after we stood up.

"Now, you go, and we'll be okay in a week or two," I told him, hoping that I was telling him the truth. He looked down at me very seriously, his handsome face so solemn I could scarcely bear it.

"I have to tell you something else," Bobo insisted. "Listen to me, Lily. I'm switching subjects here."

I nodded, reluctantly, to show him I was waiting.

"That fire was set. The fire marshal came and told Calla this morning, and she called all of us in the family. Not Lacey, naturally, but all the others. Someone tried to kill Joe C, but you stopped them."

I didn't listen to the renewed pat-on-the-back part of Bobo's speech. I was thinking about his opening sentence. I wasn't surprised by the news. In fact, I'd been taking it for granted that the person I'd seen in the yard of Joe C's house had actually started the fire. Trespasser + sudden fire = arson.

"How was it set?"

"A package of cigarettes. Not just one cigarette was lit, but a whole pack. They were left on the couch to smolder. But the flames ran away from the couch, didn't consume it, and the traces were still there."

"How is Joe C?" I asked.

He looked surprised for a minute, as though he'd been expecting me to exclaim and ask a different question.

"Nothing can kill Joe C," Bobo said, almost regretfully, pushing his hair back off his forehead. "He's like a human cockroach. Hey, I saw that twitch again!"

I looked away.

"Lily, this isn't the end of the world."

I saw I was hurting him, and I didn't want to. I didn't want to have done *any* of the things I'd done today.

And I was determined to stick to an impersonal topic.

"If Joe C had died, who would have inherited?" I asked.

Bobo turned red. "I'm not supposed to know the

answer to that, but I do," he confessed. " 'Cause I saw a copy of the will at Joe C's house. He had it stuck in the old rolltop desk. I've always loved that desk. Gee, I guess it's all burned up now. But I played with it since I was a little boy, you know, looking in the secret compartment that he'd shown me."

"The will was there?" I prodded when memories seemed to wrap him up.

"Yes. The last time I went to see Joe C . . . last week, I guess it was . . . I was sitting with Toni in the living room while Aunt Calla was helping Joe C get his shoes on after his nap. He'd asked all of the greats to come over— grandchildren, nieces and nephews. Deedra, me, Amber and Howell Three, Becca. The other three live in North Carolina. . . . So, I was showing Toni the little place you push to open the compartment. And there it was. I didn't mean anything by reading it, I promise."

After a brief period of being his sex bunny, I was now back to being Bobo's wise woman who had to approve of his actions. I sighed.

"What did it say?"

"There was lots of lawyer language." Bobo shrugged. "But what I could tell, I guess, is that Great Uncle Joe C left one thing, one furniture item, to each of us Winthrop kids. So Amber and Howell Three and I could each pick something. I was hoping I'd get the desk. I was thinking I'd try to pick first. Now everything's burned or water damaged, I guess." Bobo smiled his beautiful smile, amused at the confounding of his greed. "Of course the main thing is the house. Joe C left proceeds from the sale of the house to his great-grandchildren. Walker's three kids, and Alice Whitley's two, and Lacey's . . . oh, but . . ."

His voice trailed away. "But Deedra's dead," Bobo resumed slowly.

I digested this slowly. I thought that whom Joe C'd included was just as interesting as who he'd left out. "Nothing for Calla," I pointed out. "She's a granddaughter."

Bobo actually looked horrified. "But she's taken care of him all these years," he said.

I remembered Bobo's grandfather. He'd only been a brother-in-law to Joe C, but they were from the same mold. I wondered what Shakespearean mothers had fed men-children in those days to make them so mean.

"Did anyone know this besides you?" I asked.

"Yeah. Well, I guess I don't know," he muttered. He still seemed stunned at his great-uncle's mean-spiritedness. His thoughts must have followed the same trail mine had, because suddenly he said, "What kind of people do I *come* from?"

"You come from your parents, and they're both nice people." I had reservations about his mother, but this was no time to think about that. "Your father is a nice man," I said, and meant it. "Your grandmother is a true lady." That encompassed some less-than-desirable attributes as well as some great ones, but there again, I was always more clever at not saying things than saying them. Sometimes that was the better characteristic.

Bobo was looking a little less miserable.

"You're a good man."

"You mean that?"

"You know I do."

"That's the best thing you could've said to me." He looked down at me soberly for a long minute before his smile cracked through the serious facade. "Other than calling me your incredible stud and permanent sex slave."

All of a sudden, I felt better. I could see that the brief sexual connection we'd had had faded out of existence and that our old friendship might replace it; that we might actually forget this past twenty minutes, or at least make a good enough pretense of it.

But Jack was still coming the next day, and any reprieve from self-loathing I'd felt was washed away in the flood of anguish the idea of seeing him caused me.

Bobo raised a hand to touch my hair, or caress my neck, but something in my face stopped him.

"Good-bye, Lily."

"Good-bye," I said steadily.

He opened the front door and buttoned his suit coat to cover, at least partially, the stain on the front of his pants. He half-turned when he was almost over the threshold.

"Do you think Calla could do that?" he asked, as though he were asking a student of the dark parts of the heart. "You think she could do that to Joe C? Set the fire? The door was unlocked. She has keys."

"I think she could want him to die if she knew about the will," I told him honestly.

He was startled, but he took my word for it.

Shaking his head, he headed off down the street to find his Jeep and go home to his girlfriend and parents.

Then I was left alone with my own damn conscience.

NINE

I'd just put away my groceries when I heard a quiet knock on my front door.

Becca Whitley was there, still in brilliant makeup, though she'd changed into jeans and a T-shirt.

"You busy?" she asked.

"Come in," I said, actually relieved to have someone else break into my thoughts.

Becca had been in my house only once before, so she didn't exactly relax once she was inside. "Your boyfriend here this weekend?" she asked, standing in the middle of my tiny living room.

"Not until tomorrow. Would you like a drink?"

"Fruit juice or water," she said. "Whatever."

I poured her a glass of pink grapefruit juice, and we sat in the living room.

"Have the police been by again?" I asked, since I couldn't think of anything else to say.

"Not for a couple of days. They ask you for a list of men she'd had up there?"

"Yes."

"What'd you tell them?"

"That the men were gone before I got there in the morning."

"Naughty, naughty."

"What'd you tell them?"

"I gave them a list."

I shrugged. I didn't expect everyone to do what I did.

"I hear that the sheriff's department has an automatic door that zips open and closed all day, so much traffic is going in and out."

"You hear?" Someone's lips were awfully loose.

"Anna-Lise Puck."

Anna-Lise was Becca's workout partner. She was also a civilian employee of the sheriff's department.

"Should she be talking about that?"

"No," Becca said. "But she enjoys being in the know so much that she just can't resist."

I shook my head. Anna-Lise would find herself unemployed pretty soon. "She better watch out," I told Becca.

"She thinks she has job security."

"Why?"

"Well, she was tight with the first Sheriff Schuster." Becca shrugged. "She figures the second Sheriff Schuster won't fire her because of that."

We exchanged glances, and Becca grinned at me. Right.

"When I went to pick her up for lunch yesterday," Becca told me, "guess who I saw coming out of the door?"

I looked a question.

"Jerrell Knopp," she said significantly. "The stepfather himself."

Poor Lacey. I wondered if she knew.

"And," Becca continued, stepping on the word heavily, "our esteemed neighbor Carlton."

I was shocked. I had always figured Carlton as too fastidious for Deedra. I could feel my lips tighten in a small sneer. It just went to show.

"In fact," Becca said, "all the guys in our karate class have been in, including our esteemed *sensei*."

"Raphael? Bobo?" Raphael was the most married man I'd ever met, and Bobo was Deedra's cousin.

"Yep, and the new guys. Plus a few men that haven't been to class in a long time."

"But why?" Even Deedra couldn't have arranged a rendezvous with every single karate student.

Becca shrugged. "I have no idea."

Obviously, there was some reason, something that had been discovered during the investigation that had led to this. "Are they bringing in the tae kwon do people?" I asked.

Becca looked pleased with me. "Exactly what I asked Anna-Lise," she told me. "Yes, all the martial arts guys in Shakespeare are visiting with the sheriff. Whether or not they are really known to have known our late neighbor."

"That's quite a few men." I hesitated, then went on. "I just wonder if they'll ever find out who did kill her."

"Lily, I want the police to solve this. You know one of the men she slept with did this to her."

"Maybe."

"They hauled out lots of sheets."

"She had a drawerful of condoms." Of course, I

couldn't be sure she'd used them, but I thought fear of pregnancy would have prompted caution, if fear of disease didn't.

Becca stared at me, her eyes like bright blue marbles, while she thought that through. "So, most likely there won't be semen stains on the sheets. So, no DNA to test and compare." She'd crossed her legs, and her foot began to swing. "There may not be DNA inside her, anyway. Hey, she ever go with women?"

I returned her stare with interest, trying not to look shocked. I was learning a lot about myself today. "If she did, I never knew about it."

"Now, don't get all tight-ass, Lily," Becca said, seeing I wasn't happy with the conversation. "You know, lots of women who went through what you did would be inclined that way afterwards. Maybe Deedra had run the gamut of men, wanted something different."

"And that would be equally no one else's business," I said pointedly.

"Oh, you're no fun!" Becca recrossed her legs, picked up the morning newspaper, and tossed it down. "Well, how's old Joe C?"

"I haven't called the hospital yet, but I hear he's still alive."

"He's lucky you came along." Her narrow face was utterly sober.

"Eventually someone would have called the fire department, and the firefighters would have gotten him out."

"Well, I'm going to say thank you anyway, since Joe C is my great-grandfather."

"Did you visit him often?"

"I hadn't been to Shakespeare since I was a little kid.

But since Uncle Pardon died and I moved here, I've been by to see him maybe once every two weeks, something like that. That old rascal still likes short skirts and high heels, you know?"

"Yes, I know."

"Kind of pathetic. But he's a peppy old bastard; I'll give him that. Still capable of launching into you in the wink of an eye, you give him cause. Rip you another asshole."

"You specifically?"

"No, no. I was speaking in general. Not me."

Was I supposed to ask who? I decided not to, out of sheer perversity. "I understand you inherit, with the other great-grandchildren," I said instead, not knowing why I was commenting on what Bobo had told me.

"Yep, that's the way I hear it." Becca was smiling broadly. "But the old so-and-so isn't dead yet!" She seemed pleased to be related to such a tough bird. But then her face grew serious. "What I really came here to tell you, Lily, is that you may be getting another visit from that woman sheriff."

"Why?"

"Anna-Lise says all the karate women will come next. Because of the way Deedra died."

"How did she die?"

"She was—."

A heavy knock on the door interrupted this interesting bit of dialogue. "Too late," Becca said, almost blithely.

Before I could say anything, Becca just got up and went out my back door. I was left to answer the front with an increasingly bad feeling.

"Sheriff Schuster," I said, and it was impossible for me

to sound anything but grudging. This day had been too much for me already.

"Miss Bard," she said crisply.

Marta stepped in with Deputy Emanuel on her heels.

"Please have a seat," I said, my voice cool and insincere.

Of course, they did.

"The results of Deedra Dean's autopsy," Marta Schuster said, "were very interesting."

I raised my hand, palm up. What?

"Though various things were done to her after death"—I couldn't help remembering the glint of glass between Deedra's thighs—"she died of a single hard punch to the solar plexus." The sheriff tapped her own solar plexus by way of visual aid.

I probably looked as stumped as I felt. I finally could think of nothing to say but, "So . . . ?"

"It was a massive blow, and it stopped her heart. She didn't die from a fall or strangulation."

I shook my head. I was still clueless. Whatever reaction Marta Schuster was expecting from me, she wasn't getting it, and it was making her angry.

"Of course, it might have been an accident," Clifton Emanuel said suddenly, so we both looked at him. "It might not have been intended to kill her. Someone might have just punched her, not knowing how hard they hit."

Still I stared like a fool. I tried to understand the significance of his statement, which he had definitely delivered as though he was giving me the Big Clue.

"A hard punch," I said blankly.

They waited, with twin expressions of expectancy, almost of gloating.

118

And the shoe dropped.

"Like a *karate* strike," I said. "So . . . you think . . . what do you think?"

"The pathologist said a person would have to be strong and probably trained in order to deliver such a blow."

I felt the blood drain from my face. There was no defense against suspicion. There was no way to deny what they were simply thinking. I thought so many things at once that I had trouble sorting the ideas out. I recalled the people in my karate class, and scanned the faces in the line. Every one of the students who'd been in for more than a few months (as you can imagine, the class has a high attrition rate) had known Deedra. Raphael Roundtree had taught the math class Deedra took in high school, Carlton Cockroft had done her taxes, Bobo was her cousin, Marshall had seen Deedra trot in and out of Body Time's aerobics sessions. Though I could hardly believe it, each one could've slept with her, too.

And that was just the men. Janet had known Deedra for years, Becca was her landlady . . . and I worked for her.

I thought, *There goes my business.* I'd survived other scandals and upheavals in Shakespeare, and kept working, though not as busily as before. But if serious suspicion fell on me, I could kiss my livelihood good-bye. I would have to move. Again.

No one wants to be scared of her cleaning lady.

Schuster and Emanuel were still waiting for me to respond, and I couldn't summon a word to say. I stood. After a second of hesitation, they stood too. I walked to my door and opened it. I waited for them to leave.

They looked at each other questioningly, and then Schuster shrugged.

"We'll see you later," she said coolly, and she preceded Emanuel down my two front steps.

"I don't think so," I said, and closed the door behind them.

I sat with my hands on my knees and tried to think what to do. I could call a lawyer on Monday . . . who? Surely I knew a lawyer or two. Well, Carlton could recommend one. But I didn't want to do that, didn't want to spend the time and money to defend myself from a charge so unfounded. The sheriff's own brother was a more likely suspect than I. I figured that was why she was attaching more weight to the "karate strike" theory than it maybe deserved. How could you characterize a blow? It was what it was. If you could call a stopped heart the result of a "karate" blow, you might as well go on and say, "This strike was delivered by a right-handed student who's taken *goju-ryo* karate for approximately three years from an Asian-born *sensei.*"

If an autopsy could show Deedra had been punched while she was standing, that would surely be important. There probably weren't that many men, and even fewer women, in Shakespeare who could deliver such a blow, or who would even realize such a blow could be fatal. But if Deedra had been punched while sitting or lying down—in either case resting against a hard surface—well, that feat could be performed by a much larger pool of people.

Just at the moment I couldn't quite visualize how such a sequence of events could have occurred, but it was possible. Among the many things the sheriff had neglected to mention was Deedra's artificial violation. Was that postmortem or antemortem?

When I thought about it, a *lot* depended on the answer to that question.

And why had she been left out in the woods? It was really bad for the case for my innocence that the place she'd been dumped was off a road I frequented. There were other homes and businesses out on Farm Hill Road, sure. There was a car repair shop not a quarter of a mile beyond Mrs. Rossiter's house, and an antique/craft/flea market barn not a mile beyond that. That made me relax a little; the finger wasn't pointing so obviously at me.

Where had I been the night Deedra was killed? That would've been a Sunday. Last Sunday, though it seemed at least a month ago. Jack hadn't come that weekend; I'd done my usual chores on Saturday, the same list I was trying to complete this Saturday: two quick cleaning jobs, straightening my own house, shopping for groceries. I often followed that up by cooking for the coming week and freezing my meals. Yes, I recalled, I'd cooked Saturday night so I'd have a whole day on Sunday to do nothing much besides go work out, do some laundry, and finish a biography I'd checked out of the library.

And that had been exactly the program I'd followed on Sunday. No unexpected callers, no public appearances except the gym for an hour on Sunday afternoon. Janet and Becca had been there; I recalled speaking to both of them. I'd watched a rental movie on Sunday evening, and I'd finished the biography. No one had called. Typical Sunday evening for me.

What did all this boil down to?

I knew Deedra, and I took karate. I was somewhat familiar with the location where the body was found.

That was all.

And those same conditions applied to lots of other people.

No, I wouldn't let Sheriff Schuster get me panicked.

Not yet.

I'd automatically finished putting away my groceries, but I felt too unsettled to begin preparing my meals for the next week. It was almost suppertime, and the shadows of the tall trees in the arboretum across the street were making fringed patterns on the pavement. I tried to think of a reason to go out so I wouldn't be walking aimlessly. I decided to go see Joe C in the hospital. He didn't hear well over the telephone, anyway.

It was cool enough for a jacket. Track Street was quiet when I went out the front door. Carlton had mowed his grass for the first time, and the fresh smell released a puff of peace inside me—natural aromatherapy. That smell, when I was little, had meant home and Father and the proximity of summer. My troubles shifted, a bit; the burden was lighter.

A Bible verse flashed across my mind: "My yoke is easy, and my burden is light." The Book of Matthew, seemed like. I thought about that as I strode past Shakespeare Combined Church. After I'd been raped and scarred so horribly on my abdomen and chest, while the resulting terrible infection laid waste to my reproductive organs, my parents' minister had come to see me in the hospital. I'd sent him away. My parents had thought, maybe still thought, that I'd refused the consolation of religion because I was raging at fate. But it wasn't that I was asking, "Why me?" That's futility. Why *not* me? Why should I be exempt from suffering because I was a believer?

What had enraged me to the point of transforming my life was the question of what would happen to the men who had done such terrible things to me. My hatred was so strong, so adamant, that it required all my emotional energy. I'd shut down the parts of me that wanted to reach out to others, to cry about the pain and the fear, to be horrified because I'd killed a man. I'd made my choice, the choice to live, but it wasn't always a comfortable choice. I was convinced it wasn't the godly choice.

Now, pausing at the four-way stop a block away from the modest Shakespeare hospital, I shook my head. I always ran up against the same wall when I thought of my situation then; chained to a bed in a rotting shack, waiting for the man who'd abducted me to come claim me again, and holding a gun with one bullet. I could have shot myself; God wouldn't have liked that. I could have shot my abductor, and did; killing him wasn't good, either. I'd never thought of a third option. But in the years since then, from time to time I'd thought I might have been better off using the bullet on myself.

At that moment, in that shack, the look on his face had been worth it.

"What else could I have done?" I whispered out loud as I threaded through the cars in the hospital parking lot.

I still had no answer. I wondered what Joel McCorkindale would think of to say. I knew I'd never ask him.

Visiting hours were almost over, but the volunteer at the front desk seemed quite happy to give me Joe C's room number. Our old hospital, always in danger of closing, had been expanded and updated to suit modern medicine, and the result was a maze hard to decipher even with a floor plan. But I found the right room. There were people standing out in the corridor, talking intently in low, hushed hospital voices; Bobo, his mother, Beanie, and Calla Prader. If I had learned the family tree correctly, Calla was a first cousin of Bobo's father, once removed.

I was not ready to see Bobo again and almost spun on my heel to walk away until they'd left, but Calla spied me and was on me before I could blink.

I don't expect much from people, but I did assume she was going to thank me for saving Joe C from the flames. Instead, Calla raised her hand to slap me in the face.

I don't allow that.

Before her hand could reach my cheek, I'd gripped her wrist and held her arm rigid. We froze in a tense tableau. Then the fury seemed to drain out of Calla, taking her energy with it. The rush of angry color left her face, and even her eyes went pale and empty. When I was sure the purpose had left her, I released her wrist, and her arm dropped, dangling down by her side as if her bones had gone soft.

I looked over Calla's shoulder at Beanie and raised my eyebrows. It seemed apparent to me that Calla had just now found out about Joe C's will, and I wondered once again where she'd been when the fire started.

"I'm so sorry," Beanie said, mortified almost beyond speech. "Our whole family owes you thanks, Lily." And that must have choked her, considering the conversation we'd had when she'd terminated my employment. "Calla is just . . . beside herself, aren't you, honey?"

Calla's eyes had never left my face.

"Did you know, too?" she asked me in a low voice.

I couldn't complete that sentence mentally. I shook my head at her.

"Did you know that he's left me nothing? Did you know, too? Everyone in town seems to know that but me."

Normally I tell nothing but the truth, though I don't throw it around easily. But I could see that it was a good time to lie.

"No," I said, in a voice just as low as hers. "That makes him an old bastard, doesn't it?"

For all the violence of her feelings, that word shocked her back into herself.

Then she smiled. It wasn't a nice smile. It wasn't a middle-aged, church-going, rural-Arkansas-lady smile. Calla's smile was delighted and mean and just a wee bit triumphant.

"Old bastards," she said clearly, "have to cope for themselves, don't they?"

I smiled back. "I guess they do."

Calla Prader marched out of that hospital with a straight back and that happy, nasty smile still on her face.

Beanie stared after her, nonplussed. Beanie is in her midforties, an athletic, attractive woman whose most admirable trait is her love for her children.

"Thank you for handling that so well, Lily," Beanie said uncertainly. She was wearing a beige and white linen dress, and against her tan skin and brunette hair, the dress looked wonderful. Bobo's mother's expensive exterior hid a selfish heart and a shallow intelligence, partially concealed by good manners.

I could feel Bobo hovering on my left, but could not bring myself to look up at his face.

"Thanks, Lily," he echoed.

But his voice reminded his mother of his presence, and she turned on him like a snake about to strike.

"And *you*, young man," she began, sounding happy to have found a focus for her excited feelings, "*You* were the one who let Calla know about the will."

"I didn't know she was standing behind me," Bobo said plaintively, sounding about fourteen. "And anyway, now that we know, isn't it only honest to tell her?"

That stopped Beanie's anger like a dash of water; that question of morality, and the fact that she'd recollected that I was still standing there listening to all this family turmoil.

"Thank you for saving Uncle Joe C," Beanie said more formally. "The police tell me that you saw someone in his yard before the fire started?"

"Yes."

"But you couldn't see who it was?"

"Too dark."

"Probably some juvenile delinquent. These kids today will do anything, anything they see on television."

I shrugged. Beanie had always reduced me to gestures and monosyllables.

"But it bothers me that it was cigarettes," Beanie said, and then she sounded as if she were talking to a real person, me, instead of The Help.

I knew this from Bobo, but I had a feeling it wouldn't be wise to reveal that. "The fire was set with cigarettes?" That was expansive and unrevealing enough.

"Joe C says he didn't have any. Of course, the fire

126

marshal thought he might have set it himself, smoking in the living room. But Joe C says no. Would you like to go in and talk to him?"

"Just to see how he's doing."

"Bobo, take Lily in, please." It might have been framed as a question, but it was clearly a demand.

"Lily," Bobo said, holding open the wide door to Joe C's room. As I went by him, he lay his hand on my shoulder briefly, but I kept right on walking and kept my eyes ahead.

Joe C looked like he was a thousand years old. With the liveliness knocked out of him, he seemed like a pitiful old man. Until he focused on me and snapped, "You could have moved a little faster, girl! I got my slippers scorched!"

I hadn't spelled it out to myself, but I suddenly realized that now that Joe C didn't have a house, I didn't work for him. I felt my lips curl up. I bent down to him. "Maybe I should have just walked on by," I said very softly, but he heard every word. His face told me.

Then I squirmed inwardly. Just as his trembling jaw had meant me to. No matter how mean he was, Joe C was very old and very frail, and he would not let me forget that, would trade on it as much as he could. But I could walk away, and that was what I chose to do.

I walked away from the old man, and from his great-nephew, and I closed my heart against them both.

TEN

I was sickened by the world and the people in it, most of all by myself. I did something I hadn't done in years. I went home and went to bed without bathing or eating. I just stripped, brushed my teeth, pulled on a nightgown, and slid between my clean sheets.

The next thing I knew, I was peering at the bright numbers on the digital clock next to the bed. It was seven minutes after three. I wondered why I was awake.

Then I knew there was someone in the room with me.

My heart began that terrible pounding, but through its rhythm I heard the sounds of clothing being removed, the zipper of a gym bag, and it came to me that I was not attacking the intruder because on some level I had already recognized who was in my bedroom.

"Jack?"

"Lily," he said, and slid under the covers with me. "I took an earlier flight."

My heart slowed down a little, to a rhythm that had

more to do with another kind of excitement.

The smell of him, his skin and hair and deodorant and cologne and clothes, the combination of scents that said *Jack* filled my senses. I'd planned on making him wait to come down to Shakespeare, wait until I'd talked to him, told him I'd been unfaithful to him—sort of—so he could decide without seeing me whether or not to leave me for good. But in the private dark of my room, and because Jack was as necessary to me as water, I reached behind his head, my fingers clumsy with sleep, and worked the elastic band off his ponytail. I ran my fingers through his hair, dark and thick, separating it.

"Jack," I said, my voice sad to my own ears, "I have some things to tell you."

"Not now, okay?" he murmured in my ear. "Let me just . . . just let me . . . okay?"

His hands moved purposefully. I will say this for us; we put each other under a spell in bed together. Our troubled pasts and our uncertain future had no place in that bed.

Later, in the darkness, my fingers traced the muscles and skin and bones I knew so well. Jack is strong and scarred, like me, but his is visible all the time, a single thin puckered line running from the hairline by his right eye down to his jaw. Jack used to be a policeman; he used to be married; and he used to smoke and drink too much, too often.

I started to ask him how his case, the one that had taken him to California, was going; I thought of asking him how his friends Roy Costimiglia and Elizabeth Fry (also Little Rock private detectives) were doing. But all that really mattered was that Jack was here now.

I drifted off to sleep, Jack's breathing even and deep by my side. At eight, I woke up to the smell of coffee perking in the kitchen. Across the hall I could see the bathroom door opening, and Jack stepped out in his blue jeans and nothing else. His hair was wet and dragging over his shoulder. He'd just shaved.

I watched him, not thinking of anything, just feeling: glad to see him here in my house, comfortable with the warmth in my heart. His eyes met mine, and he smiled.

"I love you," I said, without ever meaning to, as if the sound of the words was as natural as breathing. It was something I'd held inside myself like a secret code, refusing to reveal it to anyone, even Jack, who'd devised it.

"We love each other," he said, not smiling now, but this look was better than a smile. "We have to be together more."

This was going to be the kind of conversation we needed to be dressed to have. Jack looked so clean and buff that I felt sleazy and crumpled in contrast.

"Let me get a shower. We'll talk," I said.

He nodded, and padded down the hall to the kitchen. "You want some pancakes?" he called, as though the earth had not just shifted to another axis entirely.

"I guess," I said doubtfully.

"Cut loose," he advised me as I stepped into the bathroom. "It's not every day we work up enough guts to talk about how we feel."

I smiled to myself in the bathroom mirror. It was still cloudy from Jack's shower. In it I saw a softer, gentler version of Lily; and since I'd hung it at just the right height, I couldn't see most of the scars. I avoided noticing them from long habit, avoided looking at them and thinking of what

131

my body would look like without them. I did not remember exactly what my torso had been like with no white ridges, or my breasts without circles incised around them. As I did from time to time, I caught myself regretting I didn't have something more beautiful to offer Jack, and as I did every time, I reminded myself that he seemed to find me beautiful enough.

We eyed each other cautiously as we sat down to eat. Jack had opened the kitchen window, and the cool morning air came in with a gust of smells that meant spring. I heard a car start up and glanced at the clock. Carlton was going to the Singles Sunday-school class at First Methodist, and he'd be home at twelve-fifteen, right after church. He'd change and then drive over to his mother's house for midday Sunday dinner; it would be pot roast and carrots and mashed potatoes, or baked chicken and dressing and sweet potatoes. I knew all that. I'd spent over four years learning this town and these people, making a place for myself here.

Before Jack and I even began our conversation, I knew I wasn't ready to leave. True, I had no family here in Shakespeare; true, I could clean houses as well in Dubuque (or Little Rock) as I could in Shakespeare. And true, my business had suffered a lot in the past year. But I'd won some kind of battle here in Shakespeare, and I wanted to stay, at least for now. I began to tense in anticipation of a fight.

"I don't have to live in Little Rock," Jack said. I deflated as though he'd stuck a pin in me.

"I do a lot of my work by computer anyway," he continued, looking at me intently. "Of course, I'd still need to be in Little Rock part of the time. I can keep my apartment up there, or find a smaller, cheaper one. That'd be more to the point."

We were being so careful with each other.

"So you want to live with me here in Shakespeare," I said, to be absolutely sure I was hearing him right.

"Yes," he said. "What do you think?"

I thought of what I'd done yesterday. I closed my eyes and wished a lightning bolt would hit me now, to prevent me from ever telling Jack. But that didn't happen. We'd always been honest with each other.

"I kissed someone else," I said. "I won't let you hit me, but if it'll help you feel better, you can break something."

"You kissed someone," he said.

I couldn't look at his face. "It was an after-funeral thing."

"You didn't go to bed with . . . ?"

"No." Did I really need to elaborate? Hadn't I been honest enough? Yes, I decided.

I stole a glimpse at Jack. I saw Jack's face tighten. Instead of hitting something, he looked like he himself had been hit. He was gripping the edge of the table.

"Is this someone . . . would this happen again?" he asked finally, his voice very hoarse.

"No," I told him. "Never."

Gradually, his grip on the table relaxed. Gradually, his face looked human.

"How old are you, Lily?" he asked, out of the blue.

"Thirty-one," I said. "Thirty-two, soon."

"I'm thirty-six." He took a deep breath. "We've both been through some times."

I nodded. Our names still cropped up in the news

every now and then. ("After a brutal gang rape mirroring that of Memphis resident Lily Bard's, a Pine Bluff woman was admitted to University Hospital . . ." or "Today Undercover Officer Lonny Todd was dismissed from the Memphis police force after charges he had an improper relationship with an informant. Todd is the latest in a string of dismissals in the past four years on similar charges, beginning with the firing of Officer Jack Leeds, whose relationship with the wife of a fellow officer led to her murder.")

"This is the best I've ever had it," Jack said. He was turning white as a sheet, but he went on. "You had a . . ." and he floundered there, stuck for a word.

"I had a moment of sheer stupidity."

"Okay." He smiled, and it wasn't a funny smile. "You had a moment of stupidity. But it won't ever happen again, because you said it wouldn't and you always keep your word."

I hadn't ever thought of myself as the epitome of honor, but it was true that I kept my word. I was trying not to be surprised that Jack was being so calm and level about this.

He seemed to be waiting.

"I said it wouldn't," I repeated. "And I always keep my word."

Jack seemed to relax just a little. He gave himself a little shake, picked up his fork and took a bite of his pancake. "Just don't ever tell me who," he said, not looking at me.

"You're getting so wise." Jack had a real problem with impulse control.

"It's taken me long enough." But his smile this time

134

was a real smile. "So, you never answered me."

I took a deep breath. "Yes. I want you to move in. Do you think we'll have enough room here?"

"Could I put an office in the exercise room?"

A little stunned by how easily it had been settled, I nodded silently. I'd hung a punch-and-kick bag in the middle of the second bedroom. I could live without it. I'd use the kicking pads in the aerobics room at Body Time.

Then I tried to imagine Jack sharing my bathroom fulltime. It was very small, and counter space was next to none. I wondered what we would do with his furniture. How would we divide the bills?

We had just complicated our lives enormously, and I was scared of the change. There were so many details to work out.

"You don't look very happy," Jack said. He was eyeing me from the other side of the table.

"But I am." I smiled at him, and he got that witless look on his face again. "I'm scared, too," I admitted. "Are you, a little?"

"Yeah," He confessed. "It's been a while."

"At least one of us has had prior experience. I've never done this."

Jack took a deep breath. "Would you rather just go on and get married?" he asked, every muscle in his body rigid. "That might be good, huh?"

I had to take my own deep breath while I groped for the right words to tell him what I felt. I hate explaining myself, and only the fact that I simply couldn't hurt Jack impelled me go through the discomfort of it.

"If it wasn't for other people, I would marry you today," I said slowly. "You know how happy the papers would be if they found out? You know how people would pat us on the backs and congratulate us? 'Those two poor wounded souls, they've found each other.' "

Jack's face was beginning to collapse, so I hurried on with the rest. "But that's no reason for us to bypass any happiness we can have. You know what I would really like? I'd like to be married to you with not another soul in the world knowing about it, at least until it was old news."

Jack didn't know if I'd said yes or no. He was struggling to understand. I could tell by the way he learned toward me, his eyes focused on my face.

"It would be just for us," I said, sure I'd failed in what I was trying to convey. I had always been a private person.

"Married is what you would like?"

"Yes," I said, surprised at myself. "That's what I would like."

"To be kept secret?"

"Just for a while. I'd just like to get used to it before we told anyone."

"Now?"

"No." I shrugged. "Anytime. But they put the names of people who've applied for marriage licenses in the paper. How could we get around that? Providing you . . . ?" I felt very anxious as I waited for him to speak.

"Yes," he said slowly. "I'd like that, too." He looked sort of surprised to discover that he would, though. He put his hand over mine where it was resting on the table. "Soon," he finished.

I tried to imagine that Jack did not feel about me the way I felt about him. I tried picturing Jack tiring of me in a month or two, opting for some woman in Little Rock who was more convenient and less prickly. I projected myself into that position of pain and rejection.

But I couldn't imagine it.

I didn't count on much in this life, but I counted on Jack's love. Though he'd just confessed it this morning, I'd known Jack loved me, and I'd known it with certainty.

I wasn't going to jump up and down and scream and run home to tell my mother we needed to pick out china and reserve the church. The time in my life I might have done that had long since passed by. Now that I had Jack, I had everything I needed. I didn't need the congratulations and gifts of other people to confirm that.

"Damn," Jack said, grinning like a maniac. He jumped up and began swinging his arms as if he didn't quite know what to do. "Damn!"

I felt as radiant as if I'd been painted with light. Without knowing I was standing or moving I found myself glued to Jack from head to foot, our arms wrapped around each other, the smiles on our faces too silly for words.

We'd always had electricity between us, and the high emotion we felt turned us into dynamos.

We celebrated exceptionally well.

Afterward, the kitchen was in an even worse mess. Since he'd cooked, I cleaned while Jack made the bed. Then, with the unusual prospect of a free day stretching ahead of us, we decided to take a walk together.

It was a perfect morning, both in the perimeters of our life together and in the weather outside. The spring morning was just warm enough, and the sky was bright and clear. I hadn't felt this way in years. I hadn't even come close. I was so happy it almost hurt, and I was scared to death.

After we'd gone a few blocks, I began telling Jack about Deedra. I told him about the new sheriff, and her brother; about Lacey asking me for help, and the embarassing items I'd found in Deedra's apartment; about Becca and Janet and the funeral, and the fire at Joe C's house; about the will Bobo had read when he was prying in the rolltop desk.

"Joe C's not leaving Calla anything?" Jack was incredulous. "After she's taken care of him for the past fifteen years or however long he's been too frail?"

"At least fifteen," I said. "According to what she's told me. He's leaving the more distant kids, the great-niece and great-nephews—Bobo, Amber Jean, and Howell Three, the Winthrop kids—an item of furniture apiece. Of course, that's probably not going to happen now, though there may be something worth saving in the house. I don't know. And the direct descendants are going to split the proceeds from the sale of the house."

"Who are the direct descendants again?"

"Becca and her brother, Anthony," I began, trying to remember what Calla had told me weeks before. "They descended from—"

"Just give me the list, not the begats," Jack warned me. I remembered Jack had gone to church as a child; I remembered that he'd been brought up Baptist. I wondered if we had some other things to talk about.

"Okay. Also there are Sarah, Hardy, and Christian Prader, who live in North Carolina. I've never seen them. And Deedra, who's out of the picture."

"And you think the house and lot are worth what?"

"Three hundred and fifty thousand was the figure I heard."

"Seventy thousand apiece isn't anything to sneer at."

I thought of what seventy thousand dollars could do for me.

In the newspaper, almost every day, I read about corporations that have millions and billions of dollars. On the television news, I heard about people who are "worth" that much. But for a person like me, seventy thousand dollars was a very serious amount of money.

Seventy thousand. I could buy a new car, a pressing need of mine. I wouldn't have to scrimp to save enough to pay my property taxes and my gym membership and my insurance payments, both car and health. If I got sick, I could go to the doctor and pay for my medicine all at one time, and I wouldn't have to clean Carrie's office for free for months afterward.

I could buy Jack a nice present.

"What would you like me to get you when I get seventy thousand dollars?" I asked him, an unusual piece of whimsy for me.

Jack leaned close and whispered in my ear.

"You can get that for next to nothing," I told him, trying not to look embarrassed.

We'd walked to the front of Joe C's house, and I pointed, drawing Jack's attention to the blackened front windows. Without commenting, Jack strode up the driveway and circled the house. Through the high bushes (the ones that hadn't been beaten out of shape by the firefighters) I glimpsed him at different points, looking up, looking at the ground, scoping it out. I watched Jack's face get progressively grimmer.

"You went in there," Jack commented as he rejoined me. He stood by my side, looking down at me.

I nodded, not quite focusing on him because I was assessing the damage. The upstairs looked all right, at least from the sidewalk. There was debris scattered on the yard, charred bits of this and that. When the breeze shifted direction, I could smell that terrible burned smell.

"You *went in there*," Jack said.

"Yes," I said, more doubtfully.

"Were you out of your fucking *mind*?" he said in a low, intense voice that gathered all my attention.

"It was on fire."

"You don't go *in* buildings on fire," Jack told me, and all the anger he'd suppressed this morning erupted. "You walk *away.*"

"I knew Joe C was in the house!" I said, beginning to get angry myself. I don't like explaining the obvious. "I couldn't let him burn."

"You listen to me, Lily Bard," Jack said, starting down the sidewalk almost too swiftly for me to keep up. "You listen to me." He stopped dead, turned to face me, began waving a finger in my face. I stared down at my feet, feeling my mouth begin to purse and my eyes narrow.

"When a house is on fire, you don't go in," he informed me, keeping his voice low with a visible effort. "No matter who is in that house . . . if your mom is in that house, if your dad is in that house, if your sister is in that house. If I am in that house. You. Don't. Go. In."

I took a very deep breath, kept focused on my Nikes.

"Yes, my lord," I said gently.

He threw his hands up in the air. "That's it!" he told the sky. "That's it!" Off he strode.

I wasn't about to pursue him, because I'd have to

scramble to keep up, and that just wasn't going to happen. I took off in the opposite direction.

"Lily!" called a woman's voice behind me. "Lily, wait up!"

Though I was tempted to start running, I stopped and turned.

Becca Whitley was hurrying down the sidewalk after me, her hand wrapped around the bicep of a huge man with pale curly hair. My first thought was that this man should get together with Deputy Emanuel and form a tag-team to go on the wrestling circuit.

Becca was as decorated as ever, with rhinestone earrings and lips outlined with such a dark pencil she looked positively garish. When she was in full warpaint, it was always a little jarring to remember she was so graceful and precise in karate class, and managed the apartments quite efficiently. I was pretty sure that meant I was guilty of stereotyping, something I had good reason to hate when people applied it to me.

"This is my brother, Anthony," Becca said proudly.

I looked up at him. He had small, mild blue eyes. I wondered if Becca's would be that color without her contact lenses. Anthony smiled at me like a benevolent giant. I tried to focus on my manners, but I was still thinking of Jack. I shook hands with Becca's brother and approved of the effort he made to keep his grip gentle.

"Are you visiting Shakespeare long, Anthony?" I asked.

"Just a week or so," he said. "Then Becca and I might go on a trip together. We haven't seen some of my dad's relations in years."

"What kind of work do you do?" I asked, trying to show a polite interest.

"I'm a counselor at a prison in Texas," he said, his white teeth showing in a big smile. He knew he'd get a reaction from that statement.

"Tough job," I said.

"Tough guys," he said, shaking his head. "But they deserve a second chance after they've served their sentence. I'm hoping I can get them back outside in better shape than when they came in."

"I don't believe in rehabilitation," I said bluntly.

"But look at that boy who just got arrested," he said reasonably. "The boy who vandalized Miss Dean's car last year. Now he's back in. Don't you think an eighteen-year-old needs all the help he can get?"

I looked to Becca for enlightenment.

"That boy who works over at the building supply," she explained. "The sheriff matched his voice to the one who made those phone calls to Deedra, the nasty ones. Deedra had saved the little tapes from her answering machine. They were in her night-table drawer."

Then Deedra had taken the calls seriously. And their source was a real nobody of a person, a man everyone seemed to call a boy.

I told Anthony Whitley, "See how much he learned in jail?"

Anthony Whitley seemed to consider trying to persuade me that saving the boy through counseling was worthwhile, but he abandoned the attempt before he began the task. That was wise.

"I wanted to thank you for rescuing Great-grandfather,"

he said a little stiffly, after an uneasy pause. "Becca and I owe you a lot."

I flicked my right hand, palm up; it was nothing. I glanced down the block, wondering how far Jack had gotten.

"Oh, Lily, if you could come by the apartment later, I need to talk to you about something," Becca said, so I guess I looked liked I was ready to go. I murmured a good-bye, turned in the other direction—maybe I'd follow Jack after all—rendering the two Whitleys out of sight and out of mind.

Jack was coming back. We met in the middle of the next block. We gave each other a curt nod. We wouldn't repeat the same quarrel. It was a closed subject now.

"Who was that?" he asked, looking past me. I glanced back over my shoulder.

"That's Becca Whitley, you know her," I said. "And her brother, Anthony. I just met him. Big guy."

"Hmm. Brother?"

"Yep. Anthony. Brother."

Jack put his arm around me and we strolled off as if he'd never been angry.

"They don't look much alike," he said after a moment.

"Not much, no," I agreed, wondering if I'd missed something. "Do you look like your sister?"

"No, not anything," Jack said. "She's got lots more pink in her complexion, and she's got lighter hair than I have."

We didn't talk much on our way back to my place. The fact that we loved each other seemed enough to contemplate for the moment. Jack decided he wanted to go

143

work his abs while Body Time was open, but I was awfully sore after wrestling Joe C through his bedroom window.

"I'll start your laundry if you want to go on," I said.

"You don't have to do that," Jack protested.

"It's no trouble." I knew Jack hated doing laundry.

"I'll make supper," he offered.

"Okay, as long as it's not red meat."

"Chicken fajitas?"

"Okay."

"Then I'll go by the Superette on my way home."

As Jack pulled out of my driveway, I reflected on how domestic that little exchange had been. I didn't exactly smile, but it hovered around my heart somewhere as I opened Jack's suitcase, which was really a glorified duffel bag. Jack didn't look as though he'd be neat, but he was. He had several days' worth of clothes compactly folded in the bag, and they all needed washing. In the side pockets Jack kept his time-fillers: a crossword puzzle book, a paperback thriller, and a *TV Guide*.

He always carried his own when he traveled because it saved him some aggravation. This week's was new and smooth; the one for the week just past was crumpled and dog-eared.

I was about to pitch the older one in the garbage until I realized that this was the same edition as the one missing from Deedra's coffee table. I flipped through the pages of Jack's magazine as if it could tell me something. Once more, I almost tossed it into the trash, but I reconsidered and put it on my kitchen table. It would serve as a reminder to tell Jack the odd little story of the only thing missing from Deedra's apartment.

144

As I sorted Jack's laundry, my thoughts drifted from Deedra's apartment to Becca's. She'd wanted to talk to me. I glanced down at my watch. Jack wouldn't be home for another hour, easy. I started a load of his jeans and shirts and put my keys in my pocket, locking my door behind me as I went to the apartments. It was a cooler evening after a cool day, and I wished I had thrown on a jacket. Taking the driveway to the rear of the apartment building, I strolled through the parking lot with its numbered shed—one stall for every apartment. Because it was a beautiful Sunday afternoon and because two of the apartments in the building were temporarily vacant, there were only two vehicles parked in the shed, Becca's blue Dodge and Claude's new pickup.

Looking at Deedra's empty stall, I was seized by a sudden idea. I don't like loose ends. I went into the open wood structure—really a glorified shed—and began examining the items hanging from nails pounded into the unfinished walls. Some long-ago tenant had hung tools there. Deedra had left an umbrella, and on a shelf there was a container of windshield-wiper fluid, a rag for checking the oil, an ice scraper, and some glass cleaner. I unhooked the umbrella from its nail, upended it, and out fell . . . nothing. Deedra's spare key was no longer in its usual hiding place.

I found that even more peculiar than her purse being missing from the crime scene. Her killer had known even this about Deedra, the small secret of where she kept her extra key. Now the killer could have in his possession *two* keys to Deedra's apartment, the other keys on the big ring in her purse, the other contents of the purse, and Deedra's *TV Guide*.

There didn't seem to be anything to do about this missing key. I'd tell the sheriff when I saw her next. I shrugged, all to myself.

I went to the rear door of the apartment building and stepped in. Becca's was the rear door to my left; Claude Friedrich lived in the front apartment next to it. Claude and Carrie were due to return from their mini-honeymoon this evening, and I assumed they'd go to Carrie's house permanently. Three apartments empty, then; I hoped Becca would be too busy to clean them for the next tenants. I could use some extra money.

I rapped on Becca's door. She answered almost instantly, as if she'd been standing right inside. She looked surprised.

"You said you needed to talk to me," I prompted her.

"Oh, yes, I did! I just didn't think . . . Never mind. It's good to see you." Becca stood aside to let me come in.

I tried to remember if I'd ever been in her apartment before. Becca had left it much the same as it had been in her Uncle Pardon's day. She'd just rearranged the furniture, added a small table or two, and bought a new television (Pardon had had a small, old model).

"Let me get you something to drink?"

"No, thank you."

Becca urged me to sit down, so I perched on the edge of the couch. I didn't want to stay long.

"Anthony's gone to the car wash," Becca told me. "I was sure it was him when you knocked."

I waited for her to get to the point.

"If Anthony and I do go on this trip he's planning," she began, "would you be interested in being responsible for the apartments while I'm gone?"

146

"Tell me exactly what that means."

She talked at me for some time, giving me details, showing me the list of workmen who kept a tab for the apartment-building repairs, and explaining how to deposit the rent checks. Becca was a sensible woman under all that makeup, and she explained things well.

The extra money would be welcome, and I needed the job just for the visibility. Used to be, I cleaned maybe four out of the eight apartments in the building, but that was a couple of years ago. And Pardon had hired me to clean the public parts of the building from time to time. I told Becca I'd do it, and she seemed pleased and relieved.

I stood up to go, and in that moment of silence before Becca began the courtesies of saying good-bye, I heard something upstairs.

From Deedra's apartment.

Becca said, "Well, Lily . . . ," and I raised my hand. She stopped speaking immediately, which I liked, and she mouthed, "What?" I pointed at the ceiling.

We stood looking up as if we had X-ray vision and could see what was going on overhead. Again, I heard movement in the apartment of the dead woman. Just for moment, my skin crawled.

"Is Lacey here?" I breathed, trying to catch any sound I could. Becca and I stood together like statues, but statues whose heads were rotating slightly to hear as well as possible.

Becca shook her head, and the ribbon she'd tied around the elastic band holding back her long blond hair rustled on her shoulders.

I jerked my head toward Becca's door. I looked questioningly.

147

She nodded and we went quietly across to her apartment door.

"Police?" I asked in the lowest voice that would carry.

She shook her head. "Might be family," she whispered, with a shrug.

Nothing could creep like Becca and I up those stairs. We were familiar enough with the apartment building to know what creaked and what didn't, and we were at Deedra's door before I was ready for it.

We had no gun, no weapon of any kind besides our hands, while the person inside might have an armory. But this was Becca's property, and she seemed determined to confront the intruder here and now. We both became comfortable with our stance, and I rotated my shoulders to loosen them.

Becca knocked on the door.

All movement inside the apartment stopped. There was a frozen silence as we two, hardly breathing, waited to find out what the intruder's next move would be.

That silence went on too long for Becca's taste, and she rapped on the door again, more impatiently.

"We know you're in there, and there's no way out but this door." That was true, and it made the apartments something of a fire hazard. I remember Pardon handing out rope ladders to the tenants of the second floor for a while, but he got discouraged when they all left taking the rope ladders with them, so the second floor people would just have to fend for themselves if there was a fire. I had time to remember the rope ladders while the silence continued.

More silence.

"We're not going away," Becca said quite calmly. I had

to admire her assurance. "Okay, Lily," she said more loudly, "call the police."

The door popped open as if it were on springs.

"Don't call my sister," Marlon Schuster begged.

Becca and I looked at each other simultaneously, and if I looked like she did, we looked pretty silly. Becca's bright blue eyes were about to pop out of her head with astonishment and chagrin. To trap the brother of the sheriff in such a position, in the apartment of a murder victim . . . We'd cut our own throats with our bravado. No one, but no one, would thank us for this.

"Oh, hell," Becca said, disgust in her voice. "Come down to my place."

Like a whipped puppy, Marlon slunk down to the landlady's apartment, looking smaller than ever. His black hair had been cut very short, I was guessing for the funeral, and now that I could watch him for a minute I realized that the young man was fine-boned and spare. I doubted if he could lift seventy-five pounds. I'd hoped we were catching Deedra's murderer, but now I didn't know what to think.

Without being told, Marlon sank onto the single chair that was squeezed in across from the couch. Becca and I faced him, and Becca told him to start talking.

Marlon sat staring at his hands, as if answers would sprout on them. He wasn't too far from crying.

"How'd you get in?" I asked, to get him rolling.

"Deedra gave me a key," he said, and he had a trace of pride in his voice.

"She didn't give out keys." I waited to see what he'd say next.

149

"She gave me one." The pride was unmistakable now.

Becca shifted beside me. "So why didn't you turn it in?" she asked. "I had to give the cops my key, and I own the place."

"I kept it because she gave it to me," Marlon said simply. I scanned his face for the truth. I am no human lie detector, but it looked to me like he believed what he said. I'd noticed before that Marlon was more like his father than his mother, at least as far as looks went. But Sheriff Schuster's size had been belied by his ferocious reputation as a lawman who swung his nightstick first and asked questions later. If there was a similar ferocity in his son, it was buried mighty deep.

"So, you went in with a key given you by the tenant," Becca said thoughtfully, as if she was considering the legality of his entry.

Marlon nodded eagerly.

"Why?" I asked.

Marlon flushed a dark and unbecoming shade of red. "I just wanted to . . . ," and he trailed off, aware that a sentence that began that way wasn't going to end up sounding convincing.

"You went to get . . . ?" Becca prompted.

Marlon took a deep breath. "The film."

"You and Deedra made a video?" I kept my voice as neutral as possible, but the young man flushed even deeper. He nodded, and buried his face in his hands.

"Then you're in luck, because I have all the home videos at my house," I said. "I'll go through them, and when I find yours, I'll give it to you."

I thought he would collapse from relief. Then he appeared to be screwing up his courage again. "There were

150

other things," he said hesitantly. "Mrs. Knopp shouldn't see them, you know?"

"It's taken care of," I told him.

Becca's eyes flicked from me to the boy, absorbing this information.

"You found her, Miz Bard," Marlon said. He was staring at me longingly, as if he wanted to open my head and see the images there. "What had happened to her? Marta wouldn't let me go see."

"Marta was right. If you cared for Deedra, you wouldn't have wanted to see her like that."

"How was it?" he asked, pleading.

I felt very uneasy. I tried to keep looking the boy steadily in the eyes, so he'd believe me. "She was naked in the car with no visible wounds," I said carefully. "She was sitting up."

"I don't understand."

What was to understand? The plainest explanation of the scene was probably the true one, no matter what problems I had accepting it. Deedra had had one man too many. That man had lured her out to the woods, become angry with her or simply decided she was expendable, and killed her.

"Had she been raped?" he asked.

"I don't do autopsies," I said, and my voice was too hard and angry. Deedra had been so quick to have consensual sex that it would be hard to even theorize she'd been raped unless there was a lot of damage, I was sure. Maybe the insertion of the bottle covered up damage from another source? Maybe it indicated the man couldn't perform normally?

And maybe it was just a gesture of contempt.

151

Becca told him, not unkindly, "You know, Marlon, that Deedra had lots of friends." Her tone made it clear what kind of friends Deedra had had.

"Yes, I know. But that had changed, she told me it had. Because of me. Because she really loved me and I really loved her."

I believed that like I believed Becca's hair was really blond. But everyone should have some illusions . . . well, maybe other people. I felt about a million years old as I sighed and nodded at Marlon Schuster. "Sure," I said.

"You have to believe me," he said, suddenly on fire. He straightened on Becca's chair, his eyes flashed, and for the first time I could see what Deedra had seen, the passion that made the boy handsome and desirable.

Becca said, "She told me that."

We both stared at her. Becca looked quite calm and matter-of-fact as she went on. "The last time I talked to Deedra, she told me she'd finally met someone she cared about, someone she thought she could love."

Marlon's face became radiant with relief and pride. Seeing a chance to act, I silently extended my hand and he put the key in it without thinking. I slid it out of sight, and he didn't say a word of protest.

A couple of minutes later, he left the apartment a happier man than he'd entered it. He'd been told not to worry about the video he and Deedra had made, he'd had the key removed so he no longer had that guilt weighing on him, and he'd had the ego-stroking consolation that his latest love had also loved him, enough to change her life for him.

Who wouldn't feel good?

"Did you make all of that up?" I asked Becca when the door had closed behind Marlon.

"Mostly," she admitted. "The last time I talked to Deedra, she was still complaining about the rent going up. But when I said something about seeing Marlon real often, she did say that she'd decided to be monogamous for a while."

"I wouldn't think she'd know that word," I said absently.

"Well, maybe she didn't use the term 'monogamous,' but that's what she meant."

"When was that, Becca?"

"I know exactly when that was, because the police asked me over and over. It was Saturday afternoon. We were both bringing in groceries at the same time."

"Who was here that weekend?"

"They asked me that, too. Your friend the chief of police spent the weekend over at his fiancée's. The Bickels were out of town, too, at their mother's in Fayetteville." Daisy and Dawn Bickel were twin sisters who worked at junior management level, Daisy at the local branch of a big chain of clothing stores and Dawn at Goodnight Mattress Manufacturing. "Terry Plowright was gone Saturday, to a monster truck rally somewhere on the other side of Little Rock. He didn't get in 'til about one in the morning and as far as I could tell he slept most of Sunday. He lives right across from me. That's the first floor."

I nodded.

"The upstairs front apartment by Deedra's is vacant. The one across the stairwell from her is a woman who works at Wal-Mart, and she was working most of the weekend—at least Sunday, I know, and I think some hours on Saturday. And the other front apartment is Tick Levinson, and you know how he is."

"How he is" was alcoholic. Tick was still managing to turn up to work at the local paper, where he was a pressman, but if there wasn't a dramatic intervention, Tick wouldn't be doing that in a year.

"So out of those, who do you think had anything to do with Deedra?"

"Well, Terry, for sure. He had a lot to do with her, real often. But I don't think either of them took it to heart," Becca said slowly. "Terry just isn't serious about anything besides cars and trucks. He loves being single. I don't think the Bickel twins even speak—even spoke—to Deedra, besides hello. Claude . . . well, you know, actually I think Claude might have visited Deedra once or twice, if you get my drift."

I could not have been more surprised. I was sure my face showed it.

I was disgusted, too.

"You know how men are," Becca said dryly.

I did, for sure.

"But from what Deedra said, I think it was a long time ago, maybe after he first moved back to Shakespeare from Little Rock. Before he kind of knew what was what. Right after his divorce."

Still.

"Anyway, nothing recent. And Tick? I don't think Tick lusts after anything but the next bottle, you know? You ever see him coming down the stairs after the weekend, trying to go to work? It's grim. If he smoked, I'd worry about being burned up in our beds."

That was only sensible.

"And before you ask me just like the cops did, I didn't see any strangers around that weekend, but that's not to say there weren't any. Everyone's got their own key to the outside doors." Those doors were locked at ten at night, after which the residents used their own keys.

"Speaking of keys," Becca said suddenly, and went to the desk by the door. She opened the top drawer, pulled out a key. "Here's the outside door key for when Anthony and I go on our trip."

I put it in my pocket and stood to leave as Anthony came in. He'd been to Stage, where one of the Bickel twins worked, I could see from his bag. He'd bought a lot of clothes. Getting excited about his trip, I guess.

"Where are you-all going?" I asked. I was trying to be polite.

"Oh, who can tell!" Becca laughed. "We might go to Mexico, we might go to the Dominican Republic! If we really like someplace, we might just stay there."

"You'd sell up here?"

"I think that's a possibility," Becca said, more soberly. "You gotta admit, Lily, I'm a fish out of water here."

That was true enough.

"Becca needs to see the world," Anthony said proudly.

They sure were excited. The idea of travel wouldn't make me happy at all, but I could tell Becca was ready to leave town. She'd never really been at home in Shakespeare.

I went home to find a baffled Jack squatting by the television, two stacks of tapes to his right. "Lily, would you like to tell me where you got these tapes?" he growled, staring at the episode of The Bold and the Beautiful unfolding on the screen. "Some of these are homemade porn, and some of them are *Oprah* or soaps."

I smiled. I couldn't help it. I explained about Deedra and about my desire to help by getting the tapes out of the apartment.

"I think you better tell me the whole story about Deedra from the beginning, all over again," he said. "Wasn't she that girl with no chin who lived across the upstairs hall from me?"

The previous fall, Jack had rented an apartment when he was working in Shakespeare undercover, on a job.

"Yep, that was Deedra," I told him. I sighed. The girl with no chin. What a way to be remembered. I began telling Jack, all over again, about finding Deedra in her car—the call of the bobwhite, the silence of the forest, the gray dead woman in the front seat of the car.

"So, how long had she been dead?" Jack asked practically.

"In the newspaper article, Marta is quoted as saying she'd been dead for somewhere between eighteen and twenty-four hours."

"Still got the paper?" Jack asked, and I went to rummage through my recycle bin.

Jack stretched out on the floor, pretty much filling my little living room, to read. I recalled with a sudden start that he was moving in with me, and I could look at him as much as I liked, every day. I didn't have to fill up with looking so I could replay it while he was gone. And he'd be taking up just as much space, much more often. We had a few bumps in the road ahead of us, for sure.

"So, the last one to see her was her mother, when Deedra left church on Sunday to walk home to her apartment." Jack scanned the article again, his T-shirt stretching over his back, and his muscle pants doing good things for his butt. I felt pretty happy about him being displayed on my floor like that. I felt like taking the paper away from him. Tomorrow morning he had to leave, and I had to work, and we were not making the best use of the time we had.

"I wonder what she was doing," Jack said. He was thinking things through like the former cop he was. "Did she make it home to her apartment? How'd she leave?"

I told Jack what I knew about the population of the apartment building that Sunday afternoon. "Becca was in town but I don't know exactly where she was then," I concluded. "Claude was gone, the Bickels were gone, Terry Plowright was gone. Tick, I guess, was drunk. The woman who works at Wal-Mart, Do'mari Clayton, was at the store, according to Becca."

"Where was Becca?"

"I don't know, she didn't say." I had no idea what Becca usually did on Sundays. She wasn't a churchgoer, and though she often made an appearance at Body Time, she didn't stay long. Maybe on Sunday she just slopped around in her pajamas and read the papers, or a book.

"Had that brother of hers gotten here yet?"

"No, yesterday was the first time I'd seen him."

"So he never even knew Deedra." Jack rested his chin on his hands, staring at the wood of the floor. While he thought, I fetched the old *TV Guide* from my bedroom— our bedroom—and opened it to Saturday. This would have been the one day pertinent to Deedra, since she'd died on Sunday.

I read all the synopses, checked all the sports listings,

pored over the evening shows. When Jack snapped out of his reverie long enough to ask me what I was doing, I tried to explain it to him, but it came out sounding fuzzier than it was.

"Maybe the *TV Guide* had blood on it or something, so the killer took it with him," he said, uninterested. "Or maybe Deedra spilled ginger ale on it and pitched it in the garbage. It's the purse that's more interesting. What could have been in her purse? Did she carry those big bags you could put bricks into?"

"No. Hers were big enough for her billfold, a brush, a compact, a roll of mints, and some Kleenex. Not much else."

"Her apartment hadn't been tossed?"

"Not so I could tell."

"What's small enough to be carried in a purse?" Jack rolled onto his back, an even more attractive pose. His hazel eyes focused on the ceiling. "She have jewelry?"

"No expensive jewelry. At least nothing worth staging that elaborate death scene for. If she'd been knocked on the head with a brick while she was at an urban mall, that would be one thing. She had some gold chains, her pearls, they would be worth that. But this, this arrangement in the woods . . . it seemed personal. And her pearls were there, hanging on the tree."

"Then we're back to her sex life. Who did she actually have sex with, that you know of?" Jack looked a little uncomfortable as he asked. That was sort of strange.

"Anyone she could," I said absently, beginning to think suspicious thoughts. "Do you want a list?"

Jack nodded, but kept his eyes fixed on the ceiling.

"Marcus Jefferson, that guy who used to live in the top front—the apartment you had for a while." I thought a little. "Brian Gruber's son, Claude, Terry Plowright, Darcy Orchard, Norvel Whitbread, Randy Peevely while he was separated from Heather, plus at least"—I counted on my fingers—"four others. And those are just the ones I saw there, actually saw in her apartment. But I wasn't about to give Marta Schuster a list."

"You didn't tell the police?"

"It wasn't their business. One of those men may have killed Deedra, but that's no reason for all of them to go through hell. And I'm not convinced any of them *did* kill her."

"Based on?"

"Why?" I asked, leaning forward, my hands on my knees. "Why would they?"

"Fear of exposure," Jack said, starting out assured but ending up uncertain.

"Who would fear exposure? Everyone in town knew Deedra was . . . really available. No one took her seriously. That was the tragedy of her life." I surprised myself, with my intensity and my shaking voice. I had cared more than I knew, for reasons I couldn't fathom. "Jack, were you lonely enough when you came to Shakespeare?"

Jack turned dark red. It was slow and unlovely.

"No," he said. "But it was a near thing. It was only because I thought of AIDS that I didn't. She had condoms, and I was horny, but I'd been tested and I was clean and I . . . could tell she was . . ."

"A whore?" I asked, feeling rage building up in me. And I could not understand it.

159

Jack nodded.

It's amazing how easily a good afternoon can evaporate.

"Can you tell me why you're so mad?" Jack asked my back. I was kneeling in the bathroom, scrubbing the floor by hand.

"I don't think so," I said curtly. My hands were sweating inside the rubber gloves, and I knew they'd smell like old sweat socks when I peeled the gloves off.

I was trying to figure it out myself. Deedra hadn't valued herself. That was not the fault of the men who screwed her. And she offered herself to them, no doubt about it. She asked nothing in return except maybe a little attention, a little kindness. She never asked for a long-term relationship, she never asked for money or gifts. She had wanted to be the object of desire, however fleeting, because in her eyes that gave her worth.

So could the men be considered at fault for giving her what she wanted? If something was freely offered, could you grudge the takers?

Well, I could. And I did.

And I was just going to have to swallow it. There were too many of them, among them men I liked and a very few I respected. Men just following their natures, as Deedra had been following hers. But I regretted not giving the sheriff their names. Let them sweat a little. It might be uncomfortable for them, but after all, Deedra was the one who'd suffered.

And yet, in the end, Deedra had finally found Marlon Schuster. He seemed to be a weak reed, but he wanted to be her reed. Would she have been strong enough to turn

160

her back on her way of life and stick with Marlon? Did she even care for him? Just because he offered what she'd always been searching for didn't mean she was obliged to take it.

Now we'd never know. Two years down the road from now, Deedra might've been married to Marlon, a whitewashed woman, maybe even pregnant with their child.

But that option had been taken away from Deedra, and from Marlon.

And that made me *angry*.

I felt better when the bathroom shone. I had relaxed by the time we went to bed, and as I listened to Jack's heavy, even breath beside me, I decided that somehow Jack's near-brush with Deedra absolved me of mine with Bobo. Though Jack hadn't known me well at the time, he'd known me, and now I felt as though my sin had been canceled by his.

I tossed and turned a little, unable to get to sleep. I thought of having to go to work in the morning, of Jack leaving to go back to Little Rock. I wondered if Birdie Rossiter would need me to bathe poor Durwood; I wondered if Lacey would need more help in Deedra's apartment.

Finally, it occurred to me that the remedy for my sleeplessness lay right beside me. I snuggled against Jack's back, reached over him, and began a gentle massage that I knew would wake him up in no time.

I was right.

ELEVEN

It was warmer the next day, with just a hint of the sweltering heat of summer: a wake-up call to the inhabitants of southern Arkansas.

Jack and I had gotten up early and gone to work out together at Body Time. We'd done triceps; I was sure to be sore after working triceps with Jack, because I tried heavier weights when he was with me, and I pulled harder for that extra set of reps.

Janet was there, and after she greeted Jack and went back to her leg presses, I noticed that Marshall himself came out of his office to spot her. I was pleased. Marshall needed to notice Janet, who had long had a soft spot for him.

Jack, on the other hand, would never be very partial to my *sensei* because he was well aware that Marshall and I once shared some time together. He wasn't ridiculous about it, but I noticed a stiffness in the way he chatted with Marshall.

Marshall seemed to be in a very good mood, laughing and joking with Janet, and generally going around the room in a circuit to meet and greet.

"What's up?" Jack asked when Marshall reached us.

"My ex is getting remarried," Marshall said, beaming, an expression that sat oddly on his face.

I'd had some dealings with Thea, who was tiny, lovely, and widely respected. So are small poisonous snakes.

"Who's the unlucky man?" I stood up straight after my second set of tricep pushups. Jack and I usually did them against the rack that held the heavier weights. We would put our hands close together on the top rack, and with our feet as far back as our height allowed, we would begin to lean down until our noses touched the weights, and then we'd push back up. I shook my arms to relieve the ache.

"A guy from Montrose," Marshall said, actually laughing out loud. "And I stop paying alimony when she remarries."

"When is the wedding?" Jack asked, planting his hands to do his set.

"Three months." Marshall beamed at me. "No more Thea. And he owns the John Deere dealership, so she'll be set. She's not even going to go back to work." Thea had been a child-care worker, and a very poor one, at the SCC day-care center.

"That sounds good," I said. "I hope nothing happens to the man before she marries him."

"He's in my prayers," Marshall said, and he wasn't being facetious. He slapped me on the shoulder, nodded at Jack, and strolled back over to Janet, who was patting her face with a towel. She was trying to restrain her pleasure at being singled out by Marshall, but it wasn't working. She was glowing with something besides sweat.

Back home, I showered and put on my makeup for work while Jack repacked and ate some breakfast. Then he took his turn in the bathroom while I ate some toast and made the bed.

We could make cohabiting work, I figured. It might take some adjustments, since both of us were used to living alone, and it might take some time, but we could do it.

Jack and I pulled out of the driveway at the same time, he to head back to Little Rock, and me to work for Birdie Rossiter.

Birdie was in full spate that morning. Unlike most people, who'd leave when they saw me pull up to their house, Birdie looked on me as a companion who was incidentally a housecleaner. So from the time I entered until the time I left, she provided a constant accompaniment, chattering and questioning, full of gossip and advice.

It wore me out.

I wondered if she talked to Durwood when I wasn't there. I figured Durwood qualified to be some kind of dog saint.

But sometimes, in the middle of all the inconsequential gossip, Birdie let drop a nugget of something useful or interesting. This morning, Birdie Rossiter told me that Lacey Dean Knopp had made Jerrell Knopp move out.

"I guess she's just got unhinged since poor little Deedra got killed," Birdie said, her mouth pursed in commiseration tinged with pleasure. "That Deedra, she was the light of Lacey's life. I know when Jerrell was courting her, he was mighty careful not to say one thing about Deedra. I bet he was after Lacey's money. Chaz Dean, the first husband, he died before you came to Shakespeare. . . . Well, Chaz left Lacey one nice pot of money. I knew she'd get remarried. Not just for the money. Lacey is pretty, no doubt about it, and no 'for fifty' or whatever age. Lacey is just plain pretty. If you marry somebody good-looking who has money, you just get a bonus, don't you?"

I didn't know which element would be the bonus, the money or the looks. Lacey, who had both, did not seem to me to be a particularly lucky person.

While Birdie went to pour herself another cup of coffee, I thought about Lacey making Jerrell move out, and I thought about the nasty speculation Janet and I had developed. I'd thought no one would worry if Deedra said she was going to make a relationship public, but I'd temporarily forgotten Jerrell. If she'd endangered his relationship with his wife, Deedra would have to be ruthlessly eliminated. Jerrell was crazy about Lacey. I'd never liked the man, and from my point of view it would be a great solution to Deedra's murder if her stepfather could be found guilty.

But I caught myself scowling at the sponge mop while I squeezed it out into the mopping bucket. I couldn't make a convincing case against Jerrell, no matter how much I tried. While I could see Jerrell hitting Deedra with a handy two-by-four, even taking a gun to shoot her, I couldn't see Jerrell planning the elaborately staged scene in the woods. The strewn clothes, the positioning of the body, the bottle . . . no, I didn't think so.

Birdie was back and babbling again now, but I wasn't listening. I was mentally examining what I'd just said to myself, and I was forming a little plan.

· · ·

It was a Monday eerily like that other Monday; it was clear and bright, and the air had a little touch of hotness to it, like standing just the right distance away from the burner on a stove.

Instead of parking out on Farm Hill Road, I turned into the graveled trail. I didn't want to risk my worn-out suspension on the ruts, so I parked right inside the edge of the woods. I sat in my car, just listening for a minute or two. No bobwhite today, but I heard a mockingbird and a cardinal. It was a little cooler in the shade.

I sighed and got out of my car, removing the keys and stuffing them in my pocket for safekeeping. It never hurts to be careful.

Then I was moving down the trail again, telling myself that this time there wouldn't be a car sitting in the middle of the woods, knowing there was no way a car would be in the same spot again. . . .

But there *was* a car there, parked just where Deedra's had been, and like hers it faced away from me. I stopped dead in my tracks.

It was a dark green Bronco, which explained why I hadn't picked it out before. There was someone sitting in it.

"Oh no," I whispered. I shook my head from side to side. This was like one of those dreams in which you are compelled to do something you dread doing, something you know will end in horror. When my feet began moving forward, my teeth were clenched to keep them from chattering, and my hand was over my heart, feeling it hammer with fear.

I drew abreast of the driver's window, standing well back so I wouldn't catch the smell again. I didn't think I could stand that without throwing up, and I didn't want to put myself through it. I leaned slightly to look in and then I froze. I was looking into a gun.

Clifton Emanuel's eyes were just as round and black as the barrel of the gun, and almost as frightening.

"Don't move," he said hoarsely.

I was too shocked to say anything, and I wasn't about to move a muscle. A lot passed through my mind in a second. I saw that if I acted instantly I could disarm him, though he was equally ready to pull the trigger. But he was a law-enforcement officer and my tendency was to obey him, though I knew from experience that some people in law enforcement were just as wrong headed or corrupt as the sociopaths they arrested.

On the whole. . . . I remained frozen.

"Step back," he commanded, in that eerie voice that told me he was wound as tight as a coil could be wound.

If I stepped back I wouldn't be frozen anymore, but I decided it wasn't the time to quibble with him. I stepped back. Marshall had always warned us that no matter how skilled you became in martial arts, in some situations the man with the gun would rule.

I watched, hardly breathing, as Clifton Emanuel opened the car door and emerged from the car. Though he took great care to keep the gun trained on me, there was one point at which I could've begun to move, but my uncertainty held me paralyzed.

Though I just didn't think the deputy was going to shoot, I remained tense and strung up for action. His eyes were showing a little too much white to suit me. But when I figured he'd heard me coming up the trail, drawn his gun, and sat in the car waiting for me to approach, it wasn't surprising he was squirrelly.

"Up against the car," he ordered. Now that I felt sure he wasn't going to shoot me out of hand, I began to get mad. I put my hands against the car, spread my legs, and let him pat me down, but I could feel my tolerance draining away with my fear.

He frisked me as impersonally as I could want, which was saying a lot.

"Turn around," he said, and his voice was not so hoarse.

I faced him, having to look up to gauge his emotional state from his expression. His body was relaxing a little, and his eyes looked a trifle less jumpy. I focused on looking nonthreatening, trying to keep my own muscles from tensing, trying to breathe evenly. It took a lot of concentration.

"What are you doing out here?" he asked.

He was in plainclothes, though I noticed that his khaki slacks and brown plaid shirt were not too far from the uniform in spirit.

"I could ask the same," I said, trying not to sound as confrontational as I felt. I don't like feeling helpless. I don't like that more than I don't like almost anything else.

"Tell me," he said.

"I wanted to look at the spot again because ..." I faltered, not happy at explaining what had really been an unformed feeling.

"Why?"

"Because I wanted to think about it," I finished. "See, I was thinking ..." I shook my head, trying to formulate what I wanted to say. "There was something wrong about this."

"You mean, besides the murder of a young woman?" he asked dryly.

I nodded, ignoring the sarcasm.

He lowered the gun.

"I think so too," he said. Now he looked more astonished than anything, as if it amazed him that I would think about what I'd seen that day, think about Deedra's last moments after I'd reported her death. It appeared that in Clifton Emanuel's estimation, I was so tough that the death of a woman I'd known for years wouldn't affect me. It would be wonderful, I thought, to be that tough.

He holstered his gun. He didn't apologize for drawing on me, and I didn't ask it of him. If I'd been in his shoes, I'd have done the same.

"Go on," he invited me.

"I found myself thinking that . . ." I paused, trying to phrase it so he'd understand me. "We're *meant* to think that a man came out here in Deedra's car with her."

"Or maybe arranged to meet her out here," he interjected, and I nodded, waving a hand to show I conceded that.

"Howsoever. So, she's out here, and so is the murderer, however he got here. And then, we're supposed to think that this killer got Deedra out of the car for a little sex, told her to take off her clothes. She strips for his pleasure, tossing her clothes at random, pantyhose here, blouse there, pearls, skirt . . . and she's out here in the middle of the woods naked as a jaybird. Then she has sex with him, and he's using a condom unless he's a complete moron. Or maybe they don't have sex? I don't know what the autopsy said. But at that point, something goes wrong."

Clifton was nodding his big head. "They argue about something," he said, taking over the scenario. "Maybe she threatens to tell his wife he's screwing her. But that doesn't seem likely, since everyone agrees married men didn't appeal to her. Maybe she tells him she thinks she's pregnant, though she wasn't. Or maybe she tells him he's a lousy lay. Maybe he can't get it up."

That had crossed my mind briefly before, when I'd considered Deedra's artificial violation with the bottle. When Clifton Emanuel said it, the idea made even more sense. I looked up at the deputy in surprise, and he nodded grimly. "For some people, not performing would be reason enough to go off the deep end," he told me darkly.

I looked off into the shadows of the woods and shivered.

"So he *shows* her potency," Emanuel continued. "He strikes her hard enough in the solar plexus to kill her, and while she's dying he hauls her into the car and then shoves the bottle up her . . . ah, up her." He cleared his throat in a curiously delicate way.

"And then he leaves. How?" I asked. "If he arrived in her car, how does he leave?"

"And if he came in his own car, it didn't leave any trace that we could find. Which is possible, especially if it was a good vehicle with no leaks. The ground was dry that week, but not dry enough to be powdery. Not good for tracks. But it just seems more likely that he was in the car with her, that he wouldn't risk being seen pulling in here with her. So he must've had his car already parked somewhere close. Or maybe he had a cell phone, like yours. He could call someone to come pick him up, spin some story to explain it. Someone he trusted wouldn't go the police with it."

I spared a moment to wonder why a law-enforcement officer was being so forthcoming with speculation.

"She wasn't pregnant," I muttered.

He shook his heavy head. "Nope. And she'd had sex with someone wearing a condom. But we don't know if it was necessarily the killer."

"So you think maybe he couldn't do it, and she enraged him?" But that kind of taunting didn't seem in Deedra's character. Oh, how the hell did I know how she acted with men?

"That's possible. But I did talk with a former bedmate of hers who had the same problem," Deputy Emanuel said, amazing me yet again. "He said she was really sweet about it, consoling, telling him next time would be okay, she was sure."

"That wouldn't stop some men from beating her up," I said.

He nodded, giving me credit for experience. "So that's still a possibility, but it seems more unlikely."

Emanuel paused, giving me plenty of eye contact. He had no interest whatsoever in me as a woman, which pleased me. "So," he concluded, "we're back to the question of why anyone would do in Deedra if it wasn't over some sexual matter? Why make it look like the motive was sex?"

"Because that makes so many more suspects," I said. Emanuel and I nodded simultaneously as we accepted the truth of that idea. "Could she have learned something at her job? The county clerk's office is pretty important."

"The county payroll, property taxes . . . yes, the clerk's

office handles a lot of money and responsibility. And we've talked to Choke Anson several times, both about how Deedra was at work and about his relationship to her. He looks clear to me. As far as Deedra knowing something connected to her job, something she shouldn't know, almost everything there is a matter of public record, and all the other clerks have access to the same material. It's not like Deedra exclusively . . ."

He trailed off, but I got his point.

"I'm going to tell you something," I said.

"Good," he responded. "I was hoping you would."

Feeling like this betrayal was a necessary one, I told him about Marlon Schuster's strange visit to Deedra's apartment.

"He had a key," I said. "He says he loved her. But what if he found out she was cheating on him? He says she loved him, too, and that's why she gave him a key. But did you ever find Deedra's own key?"

"No." Emanuel looked down at his enormous feet. "No, never did. Or her purse."

"What about you and Deedra?" I asked abruptly. I was tired of worrying about it.

"I wouldn't have touched her with a ten-foot pole," he said, distaste making his voice sour. "That's the only thing I have in common with Choke Anson. I like a woman who's a little more choosy, has some self-respect."

"Like Marta."

He shot me an unloving look. "Everyone else in the department thinks Marlon did it," Deputy Emanuel said quietly. He leaned back against his car, and it rocked a little. "Every single man in the department thinks Marta's blind for not bringing her brother in. They're all talking

173

against her. You can't reason with 'em. He was the last to have her, so he was the guilty one, they figure."

So that was the reason Emanuel was confiding in me. He was isolated from his own clan. "Marlon was with Deedra Saturday night?" I asked.

The deputy nodded. "And Sunday morning. But he says he didn't see her after he left to go to church on Sunday. He called her apartment several times, he says. And her phone records bear that out."

"What calls did she make?"

"She called her mother," Clifton Emanuel said heavily. "She called her mother."

"Do you have any idea why?" I asked, keeping my voice soft, because it seemed to me Clifton was about to pull the lid back on top of his loquacity, and I wanted to get everything I could out of him before the well ran dry.

"According to her mother, it was a family matter."

That lid was sliding shut.

"About Jerrell fooling around with Deedra before he dated Lacey?"

His lips pursed in a flat line, Clifton gave an ambiguous movement of his head, which could mean anything. The lid was down now.

"I'm gonna go," I said.

He was regretting talking to me now, the luxury of speculating with another skeptical party forgotten, the fact that he was a lawman now uppermost in his mind. He'd talked out of school and he didn't like himself for it. If he hadn't been so enamored of Marta Schuster, if he'd been in good standing with his fellow deputies, he'd never have said a word. And I saw his struggle as he tried to piece together what to say to me to ensure my silence.

"For what it's worth," I said, "I don't think Marlon killed her. And rumor has it that yesterday Lacey told Jerrell to move out."

Deputy Emanuel blinked and considered this information with narrowed eyes.

"And you know those pearls?"

He nodded absently.

I inclined my head toward the branch where they'd dangled.

"I don't think she would have thrown them around." The pearls had been bothering me. Clifton Emanuel made a "keep going" gesture to get me to elaborate. I shrugged. "Her father gave her that necklace. She valued it."

Clifton Emanuel looked down at me with those fathomless black eyes. I thought he was deciding whether or not to trust me. I may have been wrong; he may have been wondering if he'd have a hamburger or chicken nuggets when he went through the drive-through at Burger Tycoon.

After a moment of silence, I turned on my heel and went down the road, all too aware that he was staring after me. I didn't get that uneasy feeling with Deputy Emanuel, that prickling-at-the-back-of-the-neck feeling that some people gave me; the feeling that warned me that something sick and possibly dangerous lurked inside that person's psyche. But after our little conversation I was sure that Marta Schuster was lucky to have the devotion of this man, and I was glad I was not her enemy.

On my way into town, I was thinking hard. Now more than ever, it seemed to me—and I thought that it seemed to Clifton Emanuel, too—there was something phony about the crime scene in the woods. Though Deputy

Emanuel had run out of confidence in me before we'd run out of conversation, he too had seemed dubious about the scenario implied by the trappings left at the scene.

At my next job, Camille Emerson's place, I was lucky enough to find the house empty. I was able to keep thinking while I worked.

That implied scenario: though I'd gone over it with Emanuel, I ran it again in my head. Deedra and a flame go out to the woods in Deedra's car. The flame gets Deedra to strip, which she does with abandon, flinging her clothes and jewelry everywhere.

Then a quarrel occurs. Perhaps the man can't perform sexually, and Deedra taunts him (though Emanuel had testimony and I agreed that such taunting was unlike Deedra). Maybe Deedra threatens to tell the flame's wife, mother, or girlfriend that Deedra and the flame are having sex, period. Or possibly the flame is just into rough sex, killing Deedra in a fit of passion. But would that tie in with the catastrophic blow that stopped her heart?

I was so tired of thinking about Deedra by that time that the last explanation tempted me. I didn't want to think Deedra's death was anything more than passion of one kind or another, passion that had gotten fatally out of hand.

But as I finished dusting the "collectibles" on Camille Emerson's living-room shelves. I caught sight of myself in the mantel mirror. I was shaking my head in a sober way, all to myself.

The only injury Deedra had sustained, according to every source, was the killing blow itself. I knew all too well what rough sex was like. It's not one blow or act or bit of brutality, but a whole series of them. The object of this attention doesn't emerge from the sex act with one injury, but a series of injuries. The bottle insertion had happened after Deedra was dead. Therefore, I realized, as I carried a load of dirty towels to the laundry area, that little nasty, contemptuous act was no more than window dressing. Maybe the equivalent of having the last word in a conversation.

That said something about the person who'd performed the insertion, didn't it? I covered my hand with a paper towel and pulled a wad of bubble gum off the baseboard behind the trashcan in the younger Emerson boy's room.

So, we had someone strong, strong enough to kill with one blow. The blow was probably purposeful. Evidently, the person had *meant* to kill Deedra.

We had someone who despised women. Maybe not all women, but women in some way like Deedra. Promiscuous? Attractive? Young? All of the above?

We had someone who had no regard for human life.

And we had someone clever. When I turned it over in my mind yet again, I could see that the staging was successful if you didn't really know Deedra. Deedra wouldn't throw things around like that, even if she were stripping for someone, which I could very well imagine her doing. Even then, she might sling a blouse, but it would land on something that wouldn't tear or dirty it. She wouldn't toss her pearls around. And the woods . . . no, she wouldn't do that in the woods! Where was the lap robe or blanket for the lovers to lie on? Why ask Deedra to strip if the goal was a quick screw in the backseat of the car?

I concluded that whoever'd killed Deedra hadn't thought anything at all about her character, had only known facts: that she was promiscuous and biddable. He hadn't thought of her fastidiousness about her surroundings, hadn't thought about her care for her possessions, the care that had never extended to cover her own body.

As I closed the Emersons' door behind me, I realized that now I knew much more than I had this morning. What to do with it, how to make it work for me, was still mysterious. These pieces of knowledge were not evidence to which anyone else would give credence, but at least Clifton Emanuel had listened. I was relieved to know he had been wondering, as I had been, if the whole scene in the woods was a setup.

A setup to serve what purpose?

Okay, the purpose had to be, as the deputy and I had hinted to each other in our conversation, to misdirect. The scene had been staged to make it appear that Deedra had been killed for a sexual reason; therefore, if the scene was false, Deedra had *not* been killed because she was sexually active.

She had been killed because . . . she worked at the county clerk's office? She was Lacey Dean Knopp's daughter? She was the granddaughter of Joe C Prader? She was easily led and promiscuous, so she was an easy target? I'd hit a mental wall.

It was time to dismiss Deedra from my thoughts for a while. When I was sitting in my kitchen at noon, that was easy.

My house felt empty and bleak without Jack in it. I didn't like that at all. I ate lunch as quickly as I could, imagining him riding back to Little Rock, arriving at his own apartment. He'd return his phone messages, make notes on the case he'd just finished, answer his E-mail.

I missed him. I seemed to need him more than I ought

to. Maybe it was because for so long I had done without? Maybe I valued him more deeply because of what I'd gone through all those years ago? I saw Jack's faults; I didn't think he was perfect. And that didn't make a bit of difference. What would I do if something happened to Jack?

This seemed to be a day for questions I couldn't answer.

TWELVE

At karate class that night, I wasn't concentrating, which called down a scolding from Marshall. I was glad we didn't spar, because I would've lost, and I don't like to lose. Janet teased me as I tied my shoes, accusing me of being abstracted because I was pining for Jack. I managed to half-smile at her, though my impulse was to lash out. Allowing thoughts of a man to disrupt something so important to me was . . . I subsided suddenly.

It would be quite natural. It would be normal.

But picturing Jack in the shower wasn't what had distracted me. I'd been thinking of Deedra—her face in death, her positioning at the wheel of her red car. I didn't know what I could do to help her. I had done all I could. I finished tying my shoes and sat up, staring across the empty room at Becca, who was laughingly instructing her brother in the correct position of his hands for the *sanchin dachi* posture. She motioned me to come over and help, but I shook my head and gathered the handles of my gym bag in my fist. I was ready to be by myself.

After I got home I resumed the task of scanning Deedra's tapes, since I had promised Marlon that if I found the one that featured him I would give it to him. I found myself feeling a little sick at the idea of him keeping a video of him having sex with a woman now dead, but it was none of my business what he did with it. I disliked Marlon Schuster, though that was maybe stating my feeling for him too strongly. It was more accurate to say I had no respect for him, which was quite usual for me. I had found nothing in him to like except his tenderness for Deedra. But that was something, and I had made him a promise.

I almost dozed off as I looked at the videos. I found myself looking at things I'd never seen before: talk shows, soap operas, and "reality" shows about ambulance drivers, policemen, wanted criminals, and missing children. After viewing a few tapes I could predict what was coming next, her pattern. It was like an up-ended time capsule for the past couple of weeks in television land. When I'd transferred the videotapes into a box, the most recent ones had ended up on the bottom.

Most of the videos weren't labeled—the ones she'd already watched, I guessed. The labeled ones had abbreviations on them that only gradually began to make sense to me. I discovered that "OLTL" meant *One Life to Live* and that "C" meant *Cops*, while "AMW" was *America's Most Wanted*, and "Op" was *Oprah*.

After I'd scanned maybe ten of the tapes, I found the one of Marlon and Deedra. I only watched a second of it, enough to confirm the identity of the couple. (That was all Marlon needed, to get a tape of Deedra with another man.) I put the tape aside with a discreet Post-It.

Since I'd started the job, I kept on with it out of sheer doggedness. I was able to weed out one more home movie—Deedra and our mailman, in partial uniform. Disgusting. All the other videos seemed to contain innocuous television programming. When I got to the bottom, I realized that I could match these shows with the synopses in Jack's old magazine. These were things Deedra had taped during the week before she died. There was even an old movie Deedra had taped on Saturday morning at the end of one tape.

Deedra had had at least two tapes with previous Saturday night shows on them in her film library. She'd taped the same pattern of shows each weekend. So where was the tape from last Saturday night? She hadn't died until Sunday; she'd been alive when Marlon had left her Sunday morning, he'd said. Even if I didn't want to believe Marlon, she'd talked to her mother at church, right? So where was the Saturday night tape?

It was probably an unimportant detail, but unimportant details are what make up housecleaning. Those details add up. A shiny sink, a neatly folded towel, a dustless television screen; this is the visible proof that your house has been labored over.

I was beginning to get a rare headache. None of this made sense. I could only be glad I wasn't on the police force. I'd be obliged to listen to men tell me day after day about their little flings with Deedra, their moments of weakness, their infidelities. Surely watching a few seconds of homemade porn was better than that, if I was still obliged to clean up after Deedra in some moral way.

It was a relief when the phone rang.

"Lily!" Carrie said happily.

"Mrs. Dr. Friedrich," I answered.

There was a long pause over the line. "Wow," she breathed. "I just can't get used to it. You think it'll take people a long time to start calling me Dr. Friedrich?"

"Maybe a week."

"Oh boy," she said happily, sounding all of eighteen. "Oh, boy. Hey, how are you? Anything big happen while we were gone?"

"Not too much. How was Hot Springs?"

"Oh . . . beautiful," she said, sighing. "I can't believe we have to go to work tomorrow."

I heard a rumble in the background.

"Claude says thanks for standing up for us at the courthouse," Carrie relayed.

"I was glad to do it. Are you at your house?"

"Yes. We'll have to get Claude's things moved soon. I told my parents about an hour ago! They'd given up hope on me, and they just went nuts."

"What do you and Claude need for your wedding present?" I asked.

"Lily, we don't need a thing. We're so old, and we've been set up on our own for so long. There's not a thing we need."

"Okay," I said. "I can see that. What about me cleaning Claude's apartment after he gets his stuff out?"

"Oh, Lily, that would be great! One less thing we have to do."

"Then consider it done."

Carrie was telling Claude what I proposed, and he was objecting.

184

"Claude says that's too much on you since you clean for a living," Carrie reported.

"Tell Claude to put a sock in it. It's a gift," I said, and Carrie giggled and gave him the message.

"Lily, I'll see you soon," she said. "Oh, Lily, I'm so happy!"

"I'm glad for both of you," I said. Sooner or later, someone would tell Carrie about the fire, and she'd chide me for not telling her myself. But she didn't need to come down from her cloud of happiness and be retroactively worried about me. Tomorrow she'd be back at work and so would Claude. The lives of a doctor and a chief of police are not giddy and irresponsible.

The next morning I found myself wondering why I hadn't heard from Lacey. She'd wanted me to work some more in the apartment. Her marriage crisis must have changed her agenda, and I wasn't surprised. I worked that morning after all. The gap caused by losing Joe C as a client was filled when Mrs. Jepperson's sitter called to ask me to come over.

Mrs. Jepperson was having a lucid day, Laquanda Titchnor told me all too loudly as she let me in. Laquanda, whom I held in low regard, was the woman Mrs. Jepperson's daughter had had to settle for when better aides had all been employed.

Laquanda's greatest virtues were that she showed up on time, stayed as long as she was supposed to, and knew how to dial 911. And she talked to Mrs. Jepperson, rather than just staring at the television silently all day, as I'd seen other babysitters (of both the young and the elderly) do. Laquanda and Birdie Rossiter were sisters under the skin, at least as far as their need to provide commentary every moment of every day.

Today Laquanda had a problem. Her daughter had called from the high school to tell her mother she was throwing up and running a fever.

"I just need you to watch Mrs. Jepperson while I run to get my girl and take her to the doctor," Laquanda told me. She didn't sound very pleased I was there. It was clear to both of us we weren't exactly a mutual admiration society.

"So go," I said. Laquanda waited for me to say something else. When I didn't, she pointed out the list of emergency numbers, grabbed her purse, and hightailed it out the kitchen door. The house was still clean from my last visit, I noticed, after I cast a glance in the master bedroom at the sleeping lady. For something to do, I gave a cursory scrub to the bathroom and kitchen surfaces. Laquanda always did the laundry and dishes (what little there was to do) in between monologues, and Mrs. Jepperson was bedridden and didn't have much occasion to litter the house. Her family visited every day, either her daughter, her son, their spouses, or any of the eight grandchildren. There were great-grandchildren, too, maybe three or four.

After I'd written a brief list of needed supplies and stuck it to the refrigerator (the granddaughter would pick it up and take it to the store) I perched on the edge of Laquanda's chair set close to the bed. She'd carefully angled it so she could see the front door, the television, and Mrs. Jepperson, all in a single sweeping glance.

I'd thought Mrs. Jepperson was still asleep, but after a minute she opened her eyes. Narrowed by drooping, wrinkled lids, her eyes were dark brown and cloudy, and since her eyebrows and eyelashes were almost invisible she looked like some old reptile in the sun.

"She's really not so bad," Mrs. Jepperson told me, in a dry, rustling voice that increased her resemblance to a reptile. "She just talks to keep her spirits up. Her job is so boring." And the old woman gave a faint smile that had the traces of a formidable charm lingering around the edges.

I couldn't think of any response.

Mrs. Jepperson looked at me with greater attention.

"You're the housecleaner," she said, as if she'd just slapped a label on my forehead.

"Yes."

"Your name is . . . ?"

"Lily Bard."

"Are you married, Lily?" Mrs. Jepperson seemed to feel obliged to be social.

"No."

My employer seemed to ponder that. "I was married for forty-five years," she said after a pause.

"A long time."

"Yep. I couldn't stand him for the last thirty-five of them."

I made a strangled noise that was actually an attempt to stifle a snort of laughter.

"You all right, young woman?"

"Yes ma'am. I'm fine."

"My children and grandchildren hate me talking like this," Mrs. Jepperson said in her leisurely way. Her narrow brown eyes coasted my way to give me a close examination. "But that's the luxury of outliving your husband. You get to talk about him all you want."

"I never thought of that."

"Here I am, talking," she said undeniably. "He had an eye for other women. I'm not saying he ever actually did anything about it, but he looked aplenty. He liked stupid women."

"Then he made a mistake."

She laughed herself, after a second of thinking that through. Even her laughter had a dry and rustling sound. "Yes, he did," she said, still amused. "He did right well in the lumber business, left me enough to last out my lifetime without me having to go teach school or do some other fool thing I wasn't meant to do. 'Course, I had to run the business after he died. But I already knew a lot, and I learned more right smart."

"I guess you know who owns all the land hereabouts, since you were in lumber." It occurred to me I had a valuable source of information right here in front of me.

She looked at me, a little surprised. "I did. I used to."

"You know Birdie Rossiter, widow of M. T. Rossiter?"

"Audie Rossiter's daughter-in-law?"

"Right. Know where she lives?"

"Audie gave them that land. They built right off of Farm Hill Road."

"That's right."

"What about it?"

"There's a few acres of woods right outside the city limits sign, just south of the road."

"Hasn't been built on yet?" Mrs. Jepperson said. "That's a surprise. Less than half a mile past the city limits, yes?"

I nodded. Then, afraid she couldn't make that out, I said, "Yes."

"You want to know who that belongs to?"

"Yes, ma'am. If you know."

"You could go the county clerk's office, look it up."

"It's easier to ask you."

"Hmm." She looked at me, thinking. "I believe that land belongs to the Prader family," she said finally. "Least, it did up until maybe five years ago."

"You were working up till then?" I figured Mrs. Jepperson was in her late eighties.

"Didn't have nothing else to do. I'd make those men I hired ride me around. Let 'em know I was checking on what they were doing. You can believe I kept them on their toes. They need to keep on earning money for those worthless great-grandchildren of mine." She smiled, and if I needed another clue that she didn't really think her great-grandchildren were worthless, I got it then.

"Joe C Prader owns that land?"

"Sure does, if I remember correctly. He lets his family and friends hunt on it. Joe C's even older'n me, so he may not have any friends left. He didn't have a whole lot to start with."

Mrs. Jepperson fell asleep without any warning. It was so alarming that I checked her breathing, but she was fine as far as I could tell. Laquanda came in soon afterward and checked on the old lady too. She'd dropped her daughter off at home with instructions to take some Emetrol and ginger ale and go to bed.

"She okay while I was gone?" Laquanda asked.

"Fine. We had a conversation," I reported.

"You? And Miz Jepperson? I wish I coulda heard that," Laquanda said skeptically. "This lady knows everything, and I mean everything, about Shakespeare. At least

189

about the white folks, and a lot of the blacks, too. But she doesn't share it, no sir. She keeps her mouth shut."

I shrugged and gathered my things together. If I'd asked her about old scandals and personalities, I wouldn't have gotten the same cooperation I'd gotten in asking about land. Land was business. People weren't.

When I got back to my house to eat lunch, I had a message on my answering machine from Becca. She'd thought of a couple of bills that would come due while she was gone, and wanted to leave checks with me to cover them. After I'd eaten a tuna sandwich, brushed my teeth, and checked my makeup, I still had thirty minutes until my next appointment, so I decided to oblige.

There was a pickup truck backed in toward the rear door of the apartment building. It was half-full of boxes. Separated from Lacey or not, Jerrell was helping to empty the apartment. He wasn't anywhere in sight, so I assumed he was up in Deedra's place.

Anthony answered Becca's door. He looked as though he'd just stepped out of the shower and pulled on his clothes.

"Becca here?" I asked.

"Sure, come on in. Pretty day, isn't it?"

I nodded.

"She'll be right out. She's in the shower. We've been running," he explained.

I finally sat down to wait when a moment or two didn't produce Becca. I thought I heard the bathroom door open at one point, but if she'd peeked out she'd gone right back in. Becca was a high-maintenance woman. Her brother kept up his end of the small-talk convention with considerable determination, but I was glad when Becca showed and we could both give up. Anthony didn't seem to want to talk about anything but his experiences with the prisoners he counseled. He was on the verge of sounding obsessed, I thought.

Becca emerged from the bathroom wrapped in a robe. Even fresh from the shower, she was groomed.

"Lily," she said, surprised to see me. "When did you get here?"

"About ten minutes ago," I said.

"You should have called me," Becca told Anthony, punching him in the shoulder. "I could have hurried."

I waited for her to work her way around to the reason she'd wanted me to come over. She had arranged for the bank to send me a check for the building maintenance, and she assured me the checks would keep arriving until she returned to town and rescinded the order. She'd arranged for the utilities to be paid by automatic withdrawal, and she'd included extra in my check to pay for unexpected repairs.

Then I noticed that Anthony Whitley was looking at me a little too long, making more of a response to everything I said than it was worth. Could Becca have asked me to come over because her brother had an attraction to me? Could that have been the reason for her prolonged stay in the bathroom? The idea made me very uneasy. Some women enjoy all the male attention shown them. I am not one of those women.

I gradually worked my way out of the conversation and closer to the door. I had it half-open when Becca asked me if I had the tapes from Deedra's apartment. I nodded, and kept right on inching out of the apartment.

"If you come across a tape I'm in, would you please let me know?" Becca asked.

I stared at her, thinking of the kind of home movies Deedra had made. "Sure," I said. "But I've almost finished looking at them, and you weren't in a one. Remember, I had to go through them for Marlon?"

Becca looked puzzled. "That's funny. I borrowed Deedra's camera to tape myself doing the first five *katas* so I could see what I was doing wrong. When I returned it, I'm afraid I left the tape in the camera. I wondered if it was up there."

She looked so sincere. I was perplexed. Was she covering up in front of her brother, not wanting to say that she and Deedra had engaged in some girl-girl activities? Or was she serious about filming her *katas* so she could improve her form?

"The sheriff opened the camera and it was empty. If I come across a tape featuring you, I'll bring it over," I told her, covering all the bases. That made a good closing line, so I shut the door and turned to leave the building. I glanced down at my watch. I would be late for my next appointment if I didn't hurry.

When I looked up, there was a large, angry man standing in my way.

Jerrell Knopp looked twice as big and three times as mean when he was angry, and he was very, very upset.

"Lily, why you stickin' your nose in somebody's business?" he asked furiously.

I shook my head. This was my day for confusion. What could I have done to Jerrell?

"You gone and told the police about that day I fought

192

with Deedra, that day the boy wrote on her car."

"I did no such thing," I said promptly.

Jerrell didn't expect that. He looked at me suspiciously.

"You shittin' me, girl?" He'd certainly taken off the polite face he wore around his wife.

"I would never," I told him.

"Someone told the police that I fought with Deedra. Would you consider that morning as fighting? I told her a few home truths that she needed to hear from someone, sure enough, but as far as fighting . . . hell, no!"

That was true enough. He'd told his stepdaughter quite bluntly that she needed to keep her pants on, and she especially needed to be discreet if she was sleeping with a man of another color. He'd also, if I was remembering correctly, told her she was nothing but a whore who didn't get paid.

"I didn't tell anyone about that morning," I repeated.

"Then how come the police know about it? And why the hell did Lacey just pack my bag and tell me to go to a motel?" Jerrell's face, rugged and aging and handsome, crinkled in baffled anger.

The sheriff's department could only have found out from someone else who'd been in the apartment building at the time the quarrel had occurred. My money would be on Becca. Voices had been raised, and she lived right below Deedra. But I had my own idea about why Lacey had told Jerrell to move out. "Maybe Lacey'd heard that you slept with Deedra before you started dating her," I suggested. This was strictly a stab in the dark, but it looked like I'd hit an artery. Jerrell went white. I saw him sway as if I'd struck him. If he got any shakier, I'd have to grab hold of him so he wouldn't fall, and I didn't want to do that. I just plain didn't like Jerrell Knopp, any more than he liked me.

"Who's been saying that?" he asked me, in a choked voice that made me more worried about him than I wanted to be.

I shrugged. While he was thinking of more words, I was walking away.

I was sure he wouldn't follow me, and I was right.

There was a message on my answering machine when I returned home about five o'clock. Jump Farraclough, Claude's second-in-command, wanted me to come to the police station to sign my statement about the night I'd pulled Joe C from his house, and he wanted to ask me a few more questions. I'd forgotten all about signing the statement; too much had happened. I replayed the message, trying to read Jump's voice. Did he sound hostile? Did he sound suspicious?

I was reluctant to go to the police station. I wanted to erase the traces of Deedra Dean from my life, I wanted to think about Jack coming to live with me, I wanted to read or work out—anything, rather than answer questions. I performed a series of unnecessary little tasks to postpone answering Jump's summons.

But you don't ignore something you're told to do by the police, at least if you want to keep living and working in a small town.

Shakespeare's police station was housed in a renovated ranch-style house right off Main Street. The old police station, a squat redbrick building right in front of the jail, had been condemned. While Shakespeareans balked over raising the money to build a new station, the town police were stuck in this clumsily converted house about a block from the courthouse. This particular house had formerly been the perquisite of the jailer, since it backed onto the jail.

I came in quietly and peered over the counter to the left. The door to Claude's office was closed and the window in it was dark, so Claude hadn't yet come back to work, or maybe he'd left early. I didn't like that at all.

An officer I didn't know was on desk duty. She was a narrow-faced blonde with crooked teeth and down-slanting, tobacco-colored eyes. After taking my name, she sauntered to the partitioned rear of the big central room. Then she sauntered back, waving a hand to tell me I should come behind the counter.

Jump Farraclough was waiting in his own cubbyhole, marked out with gray carpeted panels, and the fire chief was with him. Frank Parrish looked better than he had the last time I'd seen him in his working clothes, sweating in their heat and streaked with smoke from Joe C's fire, but he didn't seem any happier. In fact, he looked downright uncomfortable.

I reminded myself there were other people in the building, while at the same time I made fun of myself for the sense of relief that gave me. Did I seriously fear harm from the assistant police chief and the fire chief? I told myself that was ridiculous.

And it might be. But I'd never feel comfortable in any kind of isolated situation with men. A glance out the window told me the sun was setting.

Jump indicated an uncomfortable straight-back chair opposite his desk. Frank Parrish was sitting to Jump's left.

"Here's your statement," Jump said brusquely. He

195

handed me a sheet of paper. It seemed like years since the fire; I barely remembered giving this statement. There hadn't been much to include. I'd been walking, I'd seen the person in the yard, I'd checked it out, I'd found the fire going, I'd extricated Joe C.

I read the statement carefully. You don't want to just scan something like that. You don't want to trust that it's really what you said. But this did seem to be in my words. I thought hard, trying to figure if I'd left anything out, trying to remember any other detail that might be important to the investigators.

No. This was an accurate account. I took a pen from the cup on the desk and signed it. I returned the pen and stood to leave.

"Miss Bard."

I sighed. Somehow I'd had a feeling this wasn't going to be that easy.

"Yes."

"Please sit down. We want to ask you a few more questions."

"This is everything." I pointed at the sheet of paper on the lieutenant's desk.

"Just humor us, okay? We just want to go over the same thing again, see if you remember anything new."

I felt wary all of a sudden. I felt my hair stand up on my neck. This wasn't just routine suspicion. They should have asked me this before I signed my statement.

"Any special reason?" I asked.

"Just . . . let's us go over this thing again."

I sat down slowly, wondering if I should be calling a lawyer.

"Now," Jump began, stretching out his legs under the

small desk, "you say that when you went to the back door at the Prader house, you used your key to get in."

"No. The door was unlocked."

"Did you ever know Joe C to leave the door unlocked at night?"

"I'd never been there at night before."

For some reason, Jump flushed, as if I'd been making fun of him.

"Right," he said sarcastically. "So, since the back door was unlocked, you didn't need to use your key. Did you have it with you?"

"I've never had a key to the Prader house." I blessed all the times Joe C had so slowly come to let me in. I blessed him for his suspicion, his crotchety nature.

Jump permitted himself to look skeptical. Frank Parrish looked off into the distance as if he were willing himself to be elsewhere.

"Your employer didn't give you a key to the property? Isn't that unusual?"

"Yes."

"But you're still sure that's what happened?"

"Ask Calla."

"Miss Prader would know?"

"She would."

For the first time, Jump looked uncertain. I pressed my advantage. "You can ask any member of his family. He always makes me wait while he comes to the door as slowly as he can manage. He really enjoys that."

Parrish turned his head to look at Jump with surprise. I began to worry even more.

"Are you planning to charge me with anything?" I asked abruptly.

"Why, no, Miss Bard."

The fire chief hadn't said anything since I'd come in. Parrish still looked uncomfortable, still sat with arms crossed over his chest. But he didn't look as though he was going to gainsay Jump Farraclough, either.

"Just tell us everything from the beginning . . . if you don't mind." The last phrase was obviously thrown in for padding, as Southern and soft as cotton.

"It's all in my statement." I was getting a feeling I couldn't ignore. "I have nothing new to add."

"Just in case you missed something."

"I didn't."

"So if someone says they saw you elsewhere, doing something else, they're mistaken?"

"Yes."

"If someone says they saw you behind the house with a gas can in your hand, instead of in front of it seeing this mysterious vanishing figure, that someone would be wrong?"

"Yes."

"Didn't you dislike Joe C?"

"Doesn't everyone?"

"Answer the question."

"No. I don't think I have to. I've made my statement. I'm leaving."

And while they were still thinking about it, I did.

I would call Carlton's cousin Tabitha if they followed me and arrested me, I decided, keeping my pace steady as I headed toward the door in the police station. Tabitha, whom I'd met once or twice when she was visiting Carlton, was an attorney based in Montrose.

Gardner McClanahan, one of the night patrol officers,

was fixing a cup of coffee at the big pot next to the dispatcher's desk. He nodded to me as I went by, and I nodded back. I'd seen Gardner the night I'd been walking, the night of the fire. I was sure that Farraclough knew that. Gardner's seeing me didn't prove anything either way except that I hadn't been trying to hide myself, but knowing he'd seen me and could vouch for at least that little fact made me feel better.

I crossed the floor, keeping my eyes ahead. Now I was almost at the front door. I tried to recall if Tabitha Cockroft's Montrose phone number was in my address book. I wondered with every step if a voice would come from behind, a voice telling me to stop, ordering Gardner to arrest me.

I pushed the door open, and no one grabbed me, and no one called after me. I was free. I hadn't realized how tense I'd been until I relaxed. I stood by my car fumbling with my keys, taking big gulps of air. If they'd put handcuffs on me . . . I shuddered when I thought of it.

Logically, there was no reason for the assistant police chief, or the sheriff, to suspect me of anything. I'd reported Deedra's death, and I'd saved Joe C's life. I'd called 911, twice, as a good citizen. But something in me persisted in being frightened, no matter how firmly my good sense told me Jump Farraclough had just been on a fishing expedition.

"Hey, Lily."

My head snapped up, and my fingers clenched into fists.

"Did you hear the news?"

Gardner was standing on the front porch, blowing on his hot coffee.

"What?"

"Old Joe C Prader died."

"He . . . died?" So that had been the reason for the requestioning. Now that the arson was murder—despite Joe C's age, surely the fire had caused his death—the investigation would have to intensify.

"Yep, he just passed away between one breath and the next while he was in the hospital."

As I'd anticipated, I'd lost another client. Shit.

I shook my head regretfully, and Gardner shook his right along with me. He thought we were both deprecating these terrible times we lived in, when an old man could have his house burned around him. Actually, I thought, if Joe C had lived in any other age, someone would have done him to death long before this.

Gardner strolled down the steps and stood beside me, looking around at the silent street, the night sky, anything but me.

"You know, they ain't got nothing on you," he said, so quietly someone a foot away from me would not have heard. "Jump just took against you, I don't know why. No one said they saw you in any backyard with any gas can. You saved that old man's life, and it ain't your fault he died of the fire. Nothing wrong with you, Lily Bard."

I took an uneven breath. "Thank you, Gardner," I said. I didn't look into his face, but out into the night, as he was doing. If we looked at each other, this would be too personal. "Thank you," I said again, and got into my car.

On my way home, I debated over calling Claude. I hated to intrude on his time with Carrie. On the other hand, they'd be married for years, and a few minutes' conversation now might save me some unpleasant encounters with Jump Farraclough. He wouldn't have tried to scare me into saying something foolish if Claude had been aware of his purpose.

Now that Joe C was dead, his estate would be divided up. I found myself speculating that the half-burned house would just be bulldozed. It was the lot that was worth so much, not the house. The arsonist had just taken a shortcut to eliminating the factor of the house and its stubborn inhabitant. Possibly he hadn't intended Joe C to die? No, leaving a very elderly man in a burning house certainly argued that the fire-starter was absolutely indifferent to Joe C's fate.

Once home, I hovered around the telephone. Finally, I decided not to call Claude. It seemed too much like tattling on the kids to Dad, somehow; a whiney appeal.

Just as I withdrew my fingers from the receiver, the phone rang.

Calla Prader said, "Well, he's dead." She sounded oddly surprised.

"I heard."

"You're not going to believe this, but I'll miss him."

Joe C would've cackled with delight to hear that. "When is the funeral?" I asked after a short pause.

"He's already in Little Rock having his autopsy done," Calla said chattily, as if Joe C had been clever to get there that fast. "Somehow things are slow up there, so they'll get him back tomorrow, they say. The autopsy has to be done to determine exact cause of death in case we catch whoever set the fire. They could be charged with murder if Joe C died as a result of the fire."

"That might be hard to determine."

"All I know is what I read in Patricia Cornwell's

books," Calla said. "I bet she could figure it out."

"Is there anything I can do for you?" I asked, to get Calla to come to the point.

"Oh, yes, forgot why I called you."

For the first time, I realized that Calla had had a few drinks.

"Listen, Lily, we're planning on having the funeral Thursday at eleven."

I wasn't going. I knew that.

"We wondered if you could help us out afterward. We're expecting the great-grandchildren from out of town, and lots of other family members, so we're having a light luncheon at the Winthrops' house after the service. They've got the biggest place of us all."

Little touch of bitterness, there. "What would you like me to do?"

"We're having Mrs. Bladen make the food, and she'll get her nephew to deliver it to the house on Thursday morning. We'll need you to arrange the food on Beanie's silver trays, keep replenishing them, wash the dishes as they come into the kitchen, things like that."

"I'd have to rearrange my Thursday appointments." The Drinkwaters came first on Thursday; Helen Drinkwater was not flexible. She'd be the only problem, I figured as I quickly ran down my Thursday list in my head. "What kind of pay are we talking about?" Before I put myself out, it was best to know.

Calla was ready for the question. The figure was enough to compensate me for the amount of trouble I'd have to go to. And I needed the money. But I had one last question.

"The Winthrops are okay with this?" I asked, my voice

carefully neutral. I hadn't set foot in the Winthrop house for five months, maybe longer.

"You working there? Honey, it was Beanie who suggested it."

I'd been the means of sending Beanie's father-in-law to jail, and she'd taken it harder than her husband, Howell Winthrop's only son. Now, it seemed, Beanie was going to sweep the whole incident under her mental rug.

For a dazzling moment, I visualized Beanie hiring me again, her friends picking me back up, the much easier financial state I'd enjoyed when she'd been my best client.

I hated needing anything that much, anything I had to depend on another person to supply.

Ruthlessly, I clamped the cord of that happiness off and told Calla that I'd call her back when I'd seen if I could arrange my Thursday schedule.

I'd be needed from around eight o'clock (receive the food, arrange the trays, wash the breakfast dishes, maybe set up the table in the Winthrop dining room) to at least three in the afternoon, I estimated. Service at eleven, out to the cemetery, back to town . . . the mourners should arrive at the Winthrop house around twelve-fifteen. They'd finish eating about—oh, one-thirty. Then I'd have dishes to do, sweeping and vacuuming . . .

When Helen Drinkwater found that by releasing me from Thursday morning, she'd be obliging the Winthrops, she agreed to my doing her house on Wednesday morning instead of Thursday. "Just this once," she reminded me sharply. The travel agent I usually got to late on Thursday I should be able to do with no change, and the widower for whom I did the deep work—kitchen and bathroom, dusting and vacuuming—said Wednesday would be fine with him, maybe even better than Thursday.

I called Calla back and told her I accepted.

The prospect of money coming in made me feel so much more optimistic that I didn't think again about my problem with Jump Farraclough. When Jack called, just as I was getting ready for bed, I was able to sound positive, and he picked up some of that glow from me. He told me he was looking into getting a smaller apartment, maybe just a room in someone's house, in Little Rock, giving up his two-bedroom apartment. "If you're still sure," he said carefully.

"Yes." I thought that might not be enough, so I tried again. "It's what I really want," I told him.

As I was falling asleep that night I had the odd thought that Joe C had already given me more happy moments in his death than he had ever given me in his life.

As if in punishment for that pleasure, that night I dreamed.

I didn't have my usual bad dreams, which are about the knife drawing designs in my flesh, about the sound of men grunting like pigs.

I dreamed about Deedra Dean.

In my dream, I was next door, in the apartment building. It was dark. I was standing in the hall downstairs, looking up. There was a glow on the landing, and I knew somehow that it came from the open door of Deedra's apartment.

I didn't want to go up those stairs, but I knew I must. In my dream, I was light on my feet, moving soundlessly and without effort. I was up those stairs almost before I knew I was moving. There was no one in the building except whatever lay before me.

I was standing in the doorway of Deedra's apartment, looking in. She was sitting on the couch, and she was lit up with blue light from the flickering television screen. She was dressed, she was intact, she could move and talk. But she was not alive.

She made sure I was meeting her eyes. Then she held out the remote control, the one I'd seen her hold many, many times, a big one that operated both television and VCR. While I looked at her fingers on the remote control, she pressed the PLAY button. I turned my head to the screen, but from where I stood I could only see an indistinct moving radiance. I looked back to Deedra. She patted the couch beside her with her free hand.

As I moved toward her, I knew that Deedra was dead and I should not get any closer to her. I knew that looking at the screen would cause something horrible to happen to me. Only dead people could watch this movie, in my dream. Live people would not be able to stand the viewing. And yet, such is the way of the subconscious; I had to walk around the coffee table and sit by Deedra. When I was close to her, I was not aware of any smell; but her skin was colorless and her eyes had no irises. She pointed again at the screen of the television. Knowing I couldn't, and yet having to, I looked at the screen.

It was so awful I woke up.

Gasping and straining for breath, I knew what I'd seen in a deathly X-ray vision. I'd seen Deedra's view. I'd seen the lid of a coffin, from the inside, and above that, the dirt of my grave.

THIRTEEN

I felt sullen and angry the next morning. I tried to trace the source of these unjustifiable feelings and discovered I was angry with Deedra. I didn't want to dream about her, didn't want to see her body again in any manifestation, dead visionary or live victim. Why was she bothering me so much?

Instead of going in to Body Time, I kicked and punched my own bag, hanging from its sturdy chain in the small room that was meant to be a second bedroom. The chain creaked and groaned as I worked out my own fears.

There'd been no semen in Deedra's body, no contusions or bruises in the genital area, only indications that she had sex at some time before she died. But in a way she'd been raped. I took a deep breath and pummeled the bag. Right, left, right, left. Then I kicked: one to the crotch, one to the head, with my right leg. One to the crotch, one to the head, with my left leg.

Okay. That was the reason, the source, of the burrowing misery that spread through me when I thought of Deedra. Whoever had jammed that bottle into her had treated her like a piece of offal, like flesh in a particular conformation with no personality attached, no soul involved.

"She wasn't much," I said to the empty room. "She wasn't much." I back-fisted the bag. I was getting tired. It hardly moved.

An empty-headed girlish woman whose sole talents had been an encyclopedic knowledge of makeup and an ability to deal efficiently with a video camera and related items, that was the sum of Deedra Dean.

I marched back to my tiny washing area and stuffed clothes in my washer. I felt something hard through the pocket of a pair of blue jeans. Still in a rotten mood, I thrust my hand into the pocket and pulled out two objects. I unfolded my fingers and stared. Keys. I labeled all keys, instantly; where'd this come from?

I shut my eyes and thought back through the week. I opened them and peered at the keys a little more. Well, one was to the apartment building doors; Becca had given it to me yesterday. The other? Then I saw another hand dropping the key into my palm, my own hand closing around it and sliding it into my pocket. Of course! This was the key to Deedra's apartment, the one she'd given to Marlon Schuster. Becca and I had made him give it up. Becca hadn't asked for it; that was unlike her. She was so careful about details. I would take it over to her.

Then I remembered I was supposed to go to the Drinkwaters' this morning instead of the next day, and I glanced at the clock. No time to stop by Becca's now. I thrust the key into the pocket of my clean blue jeans, the ones I'd pulled on for today, and I started the washer. I had to get moving if I was going to clear all my hurdles this morning.

As if to punish me for asking for a different day, Helen had left the house a particular mess. Normally, the Drinkwaters were clean and neat. The only disorder was caused by their grandchildren, who lived a few doors down and visited two or three times a week. But today, Helen hadn't had a chance (she explained in a note) to clean up the debris from the potted plant she'd dropped. And she'd left clean sheets on the bed so I'd change them, a job she usually performed since she was very particular about how her sheets were tucked. I gritted my teeth and dug into the job, reminding myself several times how important the Drinkwaters were to my financial existence.

I gave them extra time, since I didn't want Helen to be able to say I'd skimped in any way. I drove from the Drinkwaters' home directly to Albert Tanner's smaller house in a humbler part of Shakespeare.

Albert Tanner had retired on the day he turned sixty-five, and one month later his wife had dropped dead in Wal-Mart as the Tanners stood in the checkout line. He'd hired me within three weeks, and I'd watched him mourn deeply for perhaps five months. After that, his naturally sunny nature had struggled to rise to the surface of his life. Gradually, the wastebaskets had been less full of Kleenex, and he'd commented on how his phone bills had dropped when he called his out-of-town children once a week, rather than once a day. In time, the church women had stopped crowding his refrigerator with casseroles and Albert's freezer filled up with Healthy Choice microwave dinners and fish and deer he'd killed himself. Albert's laundry basket had gotten fuller as he showered and changed more often in response to his crowded social calendar. And I'd noticed that his bed didn't always need making.

As I let myself in that morning, Albert was getting ready to take his wife's best friend to an AARP luncheon.

"How does this look, Lily?" he asked me. He held out his arms and unselfconsciously offered himself up for inspection. Albert was very shaky on color coordination, a sartorial problem he'd left to his late wife, so I was often asked to give advice.

Today he'd worn a dark green golf shirt tucked into pleated khakis and dark green socks with cordovan loafers, so it was easy to nod approval. He needed a haircut, but I figured he knew that. I was only willing to give him so much monitoring. Carry it too far, it amounted to mothering. Or wifing.

In a few minutes he was gone, and I was going about my business in my usual way. I knew Albert was actually pleased I would be here when he had a solid reason to go out; he didn't like to see me work, felt uncomfortable with me moving about his house. It made him feel like a poor host.

As I was dusting the family room, where Albert spent most of his time when he was at home, I automatically began the familiar task of boxing his videos. Albert Tanner was a polite and pleasant man, and seldom made truly big messes, but he had never put a video back in its box in the months I'd worked for him. Like Deedra, he taped a lot of daytime television to watch at night. He rented movies, and he bought movies. It wasn't too hard to figure that if Albert was home, he was in front of the television.

When I finished, I had a leftover video box. A quick scan of the entertainment center came up empty; no extra tape. I turned on the VCR, and the little symbol that lit up informed me that Albert had left the tape in the machine, something he did quite often. I pushed the EJECT button, and out it slid to be popped into its container after I checked that it had been rewound. If it hadn't been, I would have left it in the machine on the off chance Albert hadn't finished watching it.

As I opened the cabinet door in the entertainment center to shelve the movies, I had a thought so interesting that I put the movies away with no conscious effort. Maybe that was where the missing tape was—the tape of Becca that she'd left in Deedra's apartment. Maybe it was in Deedra's VCR. As far as I knew, no one had turned the machine on since Deedra had been found dead.

That would be the last tape Deedra had watched. I am not superstitious, especially not about modern machinery, but something about that thought—maybe the mere fact that I'd had it—gave me the creeps. I remembered my dream all too vividly.

What it probably was, I figured as I folded Albert Tanner's laundry with precision, was the tape of Deedra's regular Saturday-night shows. She'd had company (Marlon) for Saturday night and Sunday morning, and after she'd come home from church Sunday and after she'd talked to her mother on the phone, she'd be anxious to catch up on her television viewing. She'd play her tape. Or maybe she'd had time to watch all she'd recorded and put in the tape of Becca for some reason.

I wondered if Lacey would want me back anytime soon to finish packing Deedra's things. I could check then.

The key was in my pocket.

I could check now.

I'd been so virtuous and self-protective in turning in my copy of Deedra's key to the police, but here was another key that had almost literally dropped into my hands.

Would it be wrong to use it? Lacey had given me the videos, so there should be no problem with me taking one out of the machine, presumably. The problem lay in using this set of keys to enter.

It would be better to have a witness.

I went home to eat a late-ish lunch and observed through my kitchen window that Claude was stopping in at his apartment. I watched his car turn in to the back of the building. That solved my problem, I figured; what more respectable witness could there be than the chief of police?

Claude was opening his door as I raised my hand to knock fifteen minutes later.

He jumped a little, startled, and I apologized.

"How was the trip?" I asked.

Claude smiled. "It was great to get away for a few days, and we tried a different restaurant every meal. Unfortunately, my stomach's been upset ever since." He grimaced as he spoke.

After we'd talked about Hot Springs and the hotel where he and Carrie had stayed, and about how much of his stuff he had left to pack up to move into her house, I explained my errand while Claude absently rubbed his stomach. He listened with half his usual attention.

"So," Claude rumbled in his slow, deep voice, "you think this tape is the one Becca is missing?"

212

"Might be. And she and her brother are leaving on vacation tomorrow, I guess after the funeral. Would you mind just going in the apartment with me to see?"

Claude pondered that, then shrugged. "I guess that'd be okay. All you're doing is getting the one tape. If there isn't anything in the machine?"

"Then I'll shut the door behind me and take these keys to the sheriff."

Claude glanced at his watch. "I told Jump I'd be in sometime this afternoon, but I wasn't real specific. Let's go."

As we went to the stairs, through the narrow glass panes on either side of the back door, I saw the Whitleys getting out of Becca's car. They'd been to the gym, I figured from their clothes. Becca's hair was braided. The brother and sister were talking earnestly.

By the time I heard them coming in the back door, we had unlocked Deedra's apartment and stepped in.

Half-dismantled, dusty and disordered, the apartment was silent and dim.

While Claude fidgeted behind me, I turned on the television and the VCR. The voice of the man on the Weather Channel sounded obscenely normal in the dreary living room, where a few boxes remained stacked against the wall and every piece of furniture subtly askew.

The tiny icon lit up. There was a tape in the machine. I pressed the REWIND button. Within a second or two, the reverse arrow went dark, and I pushed PLAY.

John Walsh, host of *America's Most Wanted*, filled the screen. I nodded to myself. This was one of the shows Deadra always taped. In his painfully earnest way, Walsh

213

was talking about the evening's roundup of criminals wanted and criminals caught, of the things he would show us that would make us mad.

Well. I was already mad. I started to pop the cassette out and give up on my search for Becca's tape, but instead I thought I'd fast-forward through the commercials and see if there was something else on the recording.

Ads went by at top speed. Then we were back into *America's Most Wanted,* and John Walsh was standing in front of mug shots of a man and a woman. Walsh shook his head darkly and jerkily, and the film of a crime reenactment began to play. I hit another button to watch this segment.

". . . arson," Walsh said with finality. In the reenactment clip, an attractive brunette woman with hawklike features, who somewhat resembled one of the mug shots, rang a doorbell. An elderly man answered, and the young reenactment actress said, "I'm from TexasTech Car Insurance. Your car was named by one of our insurers as being involved in an accident that dented his car. Could you tell me about that?"

The elderly man, looking confused, gestured the young woman into his living room. He had a nice home, big and formal.

The actor playing the older man began to protest that his car hadn't been involved in any accident, and when the young woman asked him if she could have an associate examine the car, he readily handed over his keys.

He was a fool, I thought.

So was I.

On the screen, the young woman tossed the keys out to her "associate," a large, blond young man with impressive shoulders. He strode off, presumably in the direction of the homeowner's garage, but the camera stayed inside the house while the owner continued expostulating with the woman. To show us how shifty this woman was, the camera dwelled on her eyes flicking around the attractive room while the homeowner rattled on. She drifted closer and closer, and when the man announced his intention of calling his own insurance agent, the young brunette dropped into a classic fighting stance, drew back her left fist into the chamber position, and struck the man in the spot where the bottom ribs come together. He stared at her, stunned, for a second or two before collapsing to the floor.

I was barely conscious of a shuffling of feet behind me.

"Excuse me, Lily," Claude said abruptly. "I'll be in the bathroom."

I didn't respond. I was too shocked.

Now the camera showed the man lying limp. He was probably meant to be dead.

"While their victim lay on his own living-room floor, breathing his last, Sherry Crumpler and David Messinger systematically looted his house. They didn't leave until they had it all: money, jewelry, and car. They even took Harvey Jenkins's rare-coin collection."

Show the mug shots again.

As John Walsh went on to detail the couple's string of similar crimes, and urged viewers to bring these two murderers to justice, their heads filled the screen once more.

I peered at the face of the woman. I paused the picture. I put my hands on either side of her face. In my imagination I painted all the colors in brightly.

"I thought I heard someone up here," Becca Whitley said from the doorway.

I hit the OFF button immediately. "Yeah, Lacey asked me to work up here some more. I shouldn't have been watching television," I said, trying to smile.

"Watching television? You? On the job? I don't believe it for a second," Becca said blithely. "I'll bet you found another tape."

She turned and spoke into the hall behind her. "Honey, she knows."

Her brother came in. He was the other mug shot. He was much more recognizable.

"Where is the real Becca Whitley?" I asked, glad they couldn't hear how loudly my heart was pounding. My knees bent slightly, and I shifted my feet for better balance. "And the real Anthony Whitley?"

"Anthony got into a little trouble in Mexico," David Messinger said. "Becca is a pile of bones in some gulch in Texas hill country."

"Why did you do this?" I asked. I waved my hand to indicate the apartment building. "This isn't riches."

"It just dropped from heaven," the woman I still though of as Becca said. "David had been romancing Becca for months when he had to leave the country for a month or two. Things were getting too hot for us to stay together. David talked Anthony into going with him. Becca was a real straight arrow, but Anthony was a bad boy. You ever wonder why the apartment building was left to just Becca? Because Anthony was in jail. In fact, that's where Dave and Anthony met. While they were down in Me-hee-co, the guys went boating together, and when the boat came back in, why, there was only one man on it. And that man

216

had all Anthony's papers." Becca smiled at me, her hard, bright smile that I'd grown nearly fond of. "I'd remade myself, as you can see. The best wig I could buy, and a lot of makeup. While I was hanging around with Becca in Dallas, being her best friend since I was gonna be her sister-in-law, she thought, her uncle died here in Shakespeare. She'd told me about him, about his apartment building and his little pile of cash. And she told me about the great-grandfather, too. I needed a place to be, a quiet place where no one would bother me. So after she'd quit her job and given up her apartment to move here, Becca and I took a little drive together."

Her smile was genuine and bright.

Sherry Crumpler and David Messinger were between me and the only door, and as I watched, David shut the door behind him. He was really big. She was really good at combat.

They were wary.

"What about the keys, did you take the keys?" How long would Claude's stomach be upset?

"I knew I'd have to give mine up to the sheriff, at least temporarily, and I couldn't be sure Deedra hadn't left some kind of message. So I stole the whole purse, and I took her extra key from the umbrella in the car stall. I came up here right when I got back from the woods, and took the *TV Guide,* because it was marked. But people started coming back from the weekend then, and I had to stay in my apartment. After that, I had a chance to come up here twice trying to find any trace she'd left about us, but I decided she hadn't left anything. Until I saw you carry out all the tapes. Then I realized she'd probably taped the show. I was watching AMW that night. You can imagine how I felt. But I was sure no one would recognize me. Then I saw Deedra on the stairs the next morning when she left for church. I was shocked when I could tell she knew who I was."

"It's incredible how much difference the makeup makes," I said, as they split up and began to approach me from both sides.

"You know, I hate the stuff," Sherry said frankly. "And I hate this damn wig. At least I could take it off to sleep, but during the day I have to wear it every minute. That time you dropped in and I was in the shower—if I hadn't trained myself to put it on perfectly the second I could, I would've strolled out of the bathroom in my bare head. But I've got discipline, and I had my hair on and my makeup in place."

She'd gradually been easing into a fighting position, her side turned toward me, her knees bent, her fists held ready. Now she struck.

But I wasn't there.

I'd stepped to the side and kicked her right knee.

She made a gagging noise, but she recovered and regained her stance. David decided to slip up behind me and circle me with his arms from behind, and I threw my head back and caught him on the nose. He staggered back and Sherry attacked again. This time her strike hit me in the ribs, and through the pain I grabbed her fist and twisted.

I was just prolonging the inevitable, but I had my pride.

I lost it when David clouted me upside my head.

"Claude!" I yelled through the ringing in my ears. "Claude!"

Becca—Sherry—was in the act of starting her kick

when Claude came out of the hall bathroom with his gun drawn. She had her back to him, but David saw him, and I was at least vaguely aware Claude was there as I shook my head to clear it. Claude managed to knock Sherry off target by shoving her shoulder, and she sprawled onto Deedra's couch while Claude kept the gun steady on David. I scrambled, minus any dignity, from between Claude and the man and woman, taking care to keep low so Claude could shoot them if he wanted to.

He spoke into his shoulder radio, got back a lot of surprise, and repeated his orders in the calm, steady, *Claude* way that kept him in office.

"I can't even leave the room, much less the town, you get in trouble," he said to me when he figured I'd gotten my breath back. "You want to tell me what this is all about?"

"She killed Deedra," I said. I opened the door David Messinger had closed, so the cops could come in. I could hear sirens coming nearer.

"Becca killed Deedra? Why?"

"She's not Becca. Deedra found that out."

The woman didn't say anything. She just glared and clutched her knee. I hoped I'd put it out on her. I hoped she was in tremendous pain. David had blood streaming from his nose, but Claude wouldn't let him reach for a handkerchief. David wasn't talking, either. Far too experienced a criminal for that.

"Well, while we chat with them about Deedra, we can book them for assault on you," Claude said thoughtfully.

"You need to watch this video." I gestured toward the VCR. "After your backup arrives," I added hastily, because I wanted Claude to stay focused on the moment.

He smiled in a grim, unamused kind of way. "Ain't a nasty video, is it?" he asked, his gaze never leaving David.

And Becca, Sherry, whatever-her-name-was launched herself from the couch. She would've flown right over the spot close to the door where I crouched if I hadn't caught desperate hold of her calf. My hands weren't large enough to get a good grip, but I slowed her down and managed to get a better one on her left ankle, the ankle of her uninjured leg. She went down half on top of me and I gathered myself and rolled. I put my forearm across her throat and she began gagging, her hands clawing at my shoulders and head. I kept my eyes shut and my head tucked, as much as was possible, and I pinned her legs with my own. I knew I had to do this myself; Claude couldn't take the gun off the bigger man.

"I'll kill you!" she said weakly.

I didn't believe she would. I believed she wanted to.

But she had tricks left. She concentrated her strength: Instead of fighting like a windmill, she fought like a trained fighter. She gripped my ears and twisted, trying to force me to roll over. I was wearing out, and wasn't as desperate as this woman, and I was going to go over any second. But I summoned the last bit of resolve I had and fisted my left hand, struggling to draw it back as far as possible. She was so intent on getting on top that she never saw what I meant to do.

I hit her in the head as hard as I could.

She made a funny noise, her grip relaxed, and her eyes went blank.

Then two men lifted me off.

It took a minute or two for things to straighten out about who the bad woman was and who the good woman was. Once Jump Farraclough and Tiny Dalton realized I was on the side of law and order (though it took some telling to convince them) they abandoned their intention of handcuffing me and instead cuffed the groggy Becca. Sherry. Whoever. Her wig had gone askew in the struggle, even as securely pinned as she'd had it. Underneath, her hair (dyed the same blond in case it happened to show, I assumed) was about an inch long. I wondered if her outstanding chest was her own, and what she would look like when the makeup was cleaned from her face; all the outlining, highlights, shadowing, and bright colors had recontoured her features until only an expert in makeup could tell what she really looked like. An expert like Deedra Dean. Deedra had seen beyond the blue contacts, the push-up bra, the paint, the wig.

"Why didn't Deedra tell someone?" Claude asked me later that day. We were sitting in his office at the police department.

"Maybe she just couldn't believe the evidence of her own eyes. She must have been still unsure about what she'd seen; maybe she wanted to look at Sherry Crumpler again, real carefully, to make absolutely sure that what she suspected was true."

"Sherry is real clever, and she doesn't seem to have any problem with killing people if half of what she told you pans out," Claude said. "I guess she figured she better kill Deedra before her partner came into town, because David is much more like he looked on TV than Sherry is. Seeing David would have clenched all Deedra's suspicions."

"Maybe they'll tell on each other," I said, my voice as tired as the rest of me was.

"Oh, they already are. They each got a lawyer from the phone book, both of whom want to make a name for themselves so they can be in the update on television. I expect to hear from *America's Most Wanted* tomorrow at the latest."

"Can you tell me what they're saying?" I wanted to be as far away from the jail and the police station and Claude as it was possible to get when the media showed up.

"David's saying they would've been out of here a week ago if Joe C had died when he was supposed to. She set the fire, of course—Sherry did. She wanted to get that $70,000 inheritance. Then she figured if David showed up claiming to be her brother, instead of her boyfriend, he'd get another share of the money. Once she'd killed Deedra, she knew she better accelerate their plan to get the money and then she better get out of town. She'd planned, he says, to sell the apartment building once they were safely away, hire someone to handle the legal work. Just send her the paper for her signature. Then she could vanish. No one would think much of it."

I examined this idea for holes, finding only a few. "She could forge the real Becca's signature?"

"Just beautiful, apparently."

"And since no one from here, including family, had seen Becca or Anthony since they were little, no one ever imagined that she wasn't Becca? It never crossed anyone's mind to question her?"

"Seems to me," Claude rumbled, "that the real Becca must have been a lonely sort of girl. I guess Sherry, in disguise, matched a superficial description of the real Becca; blond, athletic, blue-eyed. But David says the original Becca had some emotional problems, had real trouble making friends. I guess she thought David was a godsend, and when his 'sister' was willing to pal around with her, and David was already buddies with Becca's bad-ass brother, she thought her lonely days were over."

"Why did David pick a fictional job as a prison counselor?"

"Well, he'd know all about it, wouldn't he? If you'd been able to concentrate on the AMW story, you would've heard that David's been in and out of prison all his life. For that matter, Sherry too."

"She sure had a lot of nerve, living here as Becca for so long."

"It took nerve, but it was great cover. And if she could wait it out until David felt it was safe to join her, they stood to make a bunch of money—a combined $140,000 from the sale of Joe C's lot, plus what they got eventually from the sale of the apartment building. Until the story on television, which broke only days before David was due to arrive. He says she should've gotten in touch with him and made him stay away; she says she tried but he wasn't at the prearranged phone spot. So he came. On the whole, I think they felt pretty safe, pretty anonymous. Sherry's attempt to burn Joe C's house was only partly successful, but he ended up dying, and they thought it'd look funny if they left town before the funeral. But then you interfered."

"I just wanted to know what had happened to Deedra."

"According to David . . . do you really want to hear this, Lily? It's strictly what David says Sherry told him."

I nodded. I looked down at my hands so I wouldn't have to watch his face.

"Sherry drew a gun on Deedra that Sunday afternoon, a couple of hours after Deedra came home from church and encountered her on the stairs. Sherry'd done a lot of planning in those two hours, when she saw Deedra wasn't going to call the police right away. The apartment building was empty, and though she couldn't be sure someone wouldn't show up any moment, it was a risk she had to take. She had to get Deedra away from the building; if Deedra died in her apartment, the investigation might focus more on the only person around that afternoon—the landlady. Sherry got Deedra to drive out to the trail off Farm Hill Road, which Sherry knew would put them right out of the city limits, so Marta Schuster would be heading the investigation. That would complicate things real nice, since Marlon had been hanging around Deedra so much lately. Once down the track in the woods, Sherry made her stop the car and get out and strip."

I could feel my face twisting. "Made her throw her clothes."

"Yep." Claude was silent for a long time. I knew Claude was trying, and failing, as I was, to imagine how Deedra must have felt. "Then, Sherry had made Deedra strip, she backed her up against the car, and when Deedra was in place, she struck her. One blow to the solar plexus. With all she had."

I drew in a long, slow breath. I let it out.

"While Deedra was dying, Sherry forced in the bottle and positioned her in the car. It took a lot of doing, but Sherry's a martial-arts expert and a right strong woman. As you know."

I breathed in. I breathed out. "Then what?"

"Then . . . she walked home."

After all the talk about switching cars or having an accomplice, it was that simple. She walked home. If she'd stuck to the edge of the woods, she would've been all the way in town before she had to show herself. In fact . . . I tried to look at Shakespeare in my head, from an aerial view. By some careful planning, she could've come out in the fields beyond Winthrop Sporting Goods, and then it would be a stroll back to the apartments.

"Thanks to you," Claude continued after a long pause, "my wife is sitting in the house by herself, wondering when her brand-new husband is going to make it home."

I managed a smile. "Thanks to me, you're going to have your fifteen minutes of fame," I reminded him. "You caught two of 'America's Most Wanted.' "

"Because I had the trots," he said, shaking his head ruefully.

"Maybe you could leave that part out."

"I'd like to figure out a way."

"Let's say you were suspicious when we heard footsteps coming up the stairs and you concealed yourself in the bathroom so you could take them by surprise."

"That sounds better than telling them I ate some bad fish."

"True."

"Think that's the line to take."

"You got it."

"Now what, for you, Lily?"

"I have to work tomorrow." I sighed heavily, and heaved myself out of the extra chair in Claude's office. "I have to receive food and serve at Joe C's funeral."

"No, I mean . . . longer-term."

I was surprised. Claude had never asked me a question about my life.

"You know Jack is the one." I said it plainly and quietly.

"I know. He's a lucky guy."

"Well, I just see that going on."

"Think you two'll get married?"

"Maybe."

Claude brightened. "I never would have thought it. I'm glad for you, Lily."

I wondered briefly why that idea cheered Claude. Well, they say newlyweds want everyone else to get married.

" 'Cause my wife"—and he said that phrase so proudly—"called him when she found out you were involved in this showdown, and he's sitting outside in the waiting room."

"Carrie . . . called Jack?"

"She sure did. Just when you think she's a shy woman, she pulls something like that on you."

"He's here," I said, relieved beyond measure, and happier than I'd been in days.

"If you just open the door," Claude said astringently, "I wouldn't have to be telling you, you could see for yourself."

And I did.

Later that night, when the only light in my house was moonlight, I sat up in bed. Next to me, Jack lay only on his side, his hair tangling around him and his chest moving silently with his breath. His face, asleep, was peaceful and relaxed, but remote. Unknowable. I could only know the man he tried to be when he was awake. Who knew where his dreams took him, how far into his mind and heart? Farther than I could ever penetrate.

I stood, parted my curtains, and looked out the window. The lights in the upstairs apartment that had been Deedra's were still on; I guess the police had left them that way. It was a strange feeling, seeing those lights on again. On occasions I'd noticed them before, I'd always had a contemptuous reaction; *she's entertaining again,* I'd thought, and reviewed once again the host of risks she'd run in her promiscuity.

But it was not her weakness that had caused her death; it was one of her strengths that had killed her.

I wondered what that meant, what lesson could be drawn from Deedra's death. I considered for a moment, but it was either meaningless, or its moral beyond me. I remembered Deedra as she'd appeared in my dream, the remote control in her hand. Looking at a film of the inside of her coffin.

I let the curtains fall together and turned back to the bed.